TO LOVE YOU

LINDSEY HART

COPYRIGHT

Edits by Charmaine Tan.
Cover design by Cosmic Letterz.
Cover Stock Image by Wander Aguiar Photography LLC

Need to get in touch with the author?
team@lindseyhartromance.com
or
facebook.com/groups/lindseyhartromance

1

ELLIS

You know those fights between couples that are just awkward as fuck to witness? Um. Yeah. Well, I'm currently experiencing it. As a maid. Which is just a side hustle I have going on—an undercover gig, you might say—in a bid to get sweet revenge against the douchebag billionaire and his family who wrecked my dad's life.

Said fight is set to be explosive, and as the new maid—I seriously mean new since I've only been in this position for two days—I thought it would take much longer to get the juiciest bits of juice and the dirtiest bits of dirt I'm after.

When the raised voices start, I gleefully turn on the recorder I have tucked in the back pocket of my jeans—no, I don't wear a slutty maid outfit with the short little skirt and frilly white blouse or anything—and make sure I go and clean the living room first as it gets me closer to the action.

I walked in using the back door because it's sneaky, and the pin on the keyless door pad is the same as the front door, so why not? Asherly Cromwell and his fiancé, Meryl Burbank, have no idea I'm even here.

I have a feeling they wouldn't be arguing this loudly if

they knew there was someone around to hear it, though okay, it's more than a hunch. It's a straight-up fact because they care too much about appearances to do more than whisper yell at each other unless they're behind closed doors. I also know they care too much about their public image because that's exactly what the fight is about.

So, the Cromwells. They might as well be called the Asswells because that's what they are. They're assholes. And not good ones either, though assholes usually aren't. They're a killer rich family originally from England. Or at least the grandpa was. The granny is another matter. She was born and bred right here in NOLA. Her family came from old money, which was actually pretty innocent as far as old money goes. They made a fuck ton of money with patents for shoes, if you can believe it. Yes. Shoes.

As the story goes, the grandpa fell in love with more than just his wife. He loved New Orleans and decided to stay. The grandparents took some of her old family money and started a newspaper company that acquired its own publishing chain, which then expanded into a huge powerhouse publishing magazines and books. Long story short, they wrecked my dad's life by buying out his publishing company—one he'd spent his whole life working on to push things for this city and make it even better—and then literally just shutting its doors. They put everyone out of business, and bam. The end of an era. Bam, no more future for me as a journalist to work at the very paper that made me want to do this job in the first place. Bam, they promised they wouldn't shut the doors, but they went back on their word. Bam, all my dad's pride and joy down the drain. Bam, instant spiral into a very terrible depression. Bam, bang, bing, bong, bam. All of that added together is an excellent

recipe for revenge, which is better served juicy and piping hot, as people say.

They're right, you know. I imagine revenge as a delicious, steamy pie pulled straight from the oven with the fragrant scent of peaches—because they're my favorite—and sugary zest you can just about taste simply by inhaling it to the back of your throat, filling up the entire house. Yeah, that's revenge.

So, that's why I'm here cleaning this freaking palace of a house owned by freaking Asherly Cromwell. He's the next generation and one of the heirs to the newspaper and magazine empire—heirs who did absolutely fucking nothing because they didn't have to. That's the nice thing about being an heir. There are five cousins—four boys and one girl. And they're all spoiled, rotten, and nasty bad apples that would make the worst revenge pie if they were cut up and baked into it. *Ewwwww.* People pie is definitely not my thing. But, back to Ash Cromwell.

He hates the name Asherly, obviously, so he goes by Ash. He's the oldest, and he wasn't my target in particular since he seemed quite normal and the least likely to have some dirt going on that I could undercover my ass and find, but it just so happened he was hiring a new maid, so presto change. I changed my ass from a journalist to a cleaner and got myself hired thanks to some stellar fake references provided by my boss, who is most eager to get some sleaze. Yes, I'm technically a bit of a dirtbag reporter myself, but it isn't what I want to do with the rest of my life. The path to leaving this life of crime and dirt will end with revenge. The Cromwells are so going down.

Anyway, right, back to the current fight.

I get down on my hands and knees in the living room, bust out a scrub brush and towel, and start working on an

imaginary stain on the hardwood floor in the living room right in front of the couch. This means that from the spiral staircase about forty feet away or maybe more—because this place is truly castle-style huge and antique-looking, even though there are a bunch of modern updates which were thrown in—Ash and Meryl can't see me.

"Meryl, come on. I'm not giving you the ring. You know all about the curse."

"I don't believe in curses." Meryl has a high-pitched kind of screamy-sounding voice that matches the resting bitch face she usually has going on.

Maybe I'm just jealous because Meryl is definitely a ten from her stacked body with perfect breasts to her wild mane of dyed blonde hair. She's also the daughter of a big newspaper baron who lives in New York, and she lives there too. She's just here because she and Ash met at some conference or family dinner or whatever the fuck rich people do to socialize, and they fell in love and are dating now. Meryl is the kind of woman who can rock the shit out of a power suit, and that's saying a lot.

I peek up from behind the couch, where I can see Meryl at the top of the staircase. She flips her blonde hair over her shoulder and lets out an exasperated sigh. She's wearing a hot pink power suit and pink heels to match—the super thin kind of heel that only a woman with feet of steel can pull off.

"Good god, Ash, you're way too old for that kind of thing. Plus, you told me you don't believe in it either. You said you think it's stupid. You, your brother, and all your cousins made that crazy pact just to rile your grandma up for her curses."

Curses? What's this about curses? I refrain from moving to check my recorder because that would mean pulling it out

and giving myself away. I'm very confident it's recording as it's never let me down before. I'm practically salivating at this unexpected bit of juicy, delicious bullshit I can most definitely work with. God, this will make one hell of a story.

Eat my ass, you Asswells.

"Meryl..." Ash starts using that deep tone of voice guys use when they're trying to be calm and rational on the outside because they don't want to come off as being a jerk, but inside they're actually total jerks. "I told you about that because I wanted to try and explain to you why a traditional marriage would never work for me. We were both hammered."

"But you still said you didn't believe in it. If I recall it well, you said that your grandma's heart was broken when both her sons got messy divorces, and she went to a fortune-teller—"

"Not a fortune teller."

"Well, what would you call a lady who does tarot readings?"

Ash sighs hard, and more of his inner jerk leaks out. "Anyway, yes, okay, she had five heirlooms blessed by this lady. And by blessed, I mean cursed. Each one is supposed to help the five of us—my cousins, my brother, and me—meet our soulmates. But seriously, in this day and age, who would believe in a curse like this? However, it's Granny we are talking about, and when Granny says something is cursed, you better believe it because that woman does not joke around. It's also why I can't give it to you."

"Meryl, this marriage between us is just for show, so my grandmother will leave me the heck alone, and your dad can stop pestering you. It's good for business. When we want to get a divorce, we can go our own ways. The business will not suffer since the marriage won't be real. People will eat it up, though. Everyone loves marriage gossip, but they love divorce even more, so we'll get the double zinger. Two big events."

God, the Cromwells really are crazier than I knew. That's what too much money does to a person. It like... fucks your brain or something.

"Yes, this is a marriage of convenience." Meryl actually seems kind of bored by now, and that makes two of us. "Yes, it will give us a few years of peace while we fake it, and then we can go our own ways. Also, you're right. It's good for business all around. The magazines, papers, the online stuff. All of it. When we get divorced, we can say we tried, and we'll be a few years older by then, so maybe the focus can shift off of us and onto one of your cousins, or brother, or something. Your grandma will stop hounding you, and my dad can give up on grandchildren for good. It's going to work out whether I'm your soulmate or not. So—"

"I still can't give you the ring."

"Why? Because you're afraid of being stuck with me forever? If it's a real marriage, and you want it to look real, wouldn't your granny be suspicious if you *didn't* give me the ring?"

"We have a week before we announce we're engaged. I'm going to take the ring to a jeweler who does custom work and get them to make a duplicate."

"That's crazy."

"It might be crazy," Ash bites out, "But I'm not taking the chance."

"Says the man who says he's too grown up for curses and nonsense like this, who says he won't let his life be ruled by his granny's crazy theories, who inherited that ring years ago and just kept it sitting in a box in his house. Were you maybe waiting for it to guide you like a freaking magic compass to the love of your life? Well, it's laughable because you made a pact with your brother and cousins to never fall in love. Because love is nonsense, and everyone knows monogamy and old-fashioned notions of two people being together for life don't work in modern society. Your parents, aunt and uncle were fine examples for you guys I'm sure."

Ba-zing! Dang. I give serious props to Meryl right now. I didn't like her at first sight because she was blonde and too pretty, and she looked like a ditz, but she's honestly pretty smart. She does need to lady-up and use real swears, though. Freaking doesn't exactly cut it in my books. Not that I go around dropping cuss words anywhere except in my head because I know how childish it makes a person look. Maybe she's the same in that she says it in her brain but filters it with her mouth.

But also, seriously??? A fake marriage? How great does it get? This is going to make for the best story ever if I play my cards right. I have it recorded too, so they can't even deny it. Good gravy—ha, now who's using non-swearing euphemisms—I wonder if this could land me some serious cash. I could sell this story to some rag who wants to be the first to break it. Asherly Cromwell and Meryl Burbank are rich, so it makes them fair game. People like reading about the rich being sneaky, scammy, and bad more than they like to read about happy marriages and philanthropy.

"Do you really have it here?" Meryl suddenly asks. "The ring?"

"Yes..." Ash trails off, belatedly realizing his mistake. "I have it."

"Can you get it? I want to see it. I want to just...I don't know. I want to look at it. I want to see if it really is cursed."

"Neither of us believe that."

"But still, you clearly kind of do because you've made

pacts related to it. One, don't fall in love because love isn't real. And two, don't let your life be ruled by crazy cursed heirlooms that your granny hands out willy nilly."

"Meryl..."

"Please? Just let me see it, and I'll go. I have to catch a flight in a few hours back to New York anyway. Let me just look at it, and I promise I'll never bring it up again—not the ring, not the curse, nothing. I'll be back next week, and you'll have the new ring ready. Then, we can announce our engagement and get ready to live the next few years with radio silence and zero interference in our personal lives from overbearing family members."

I guess it doesn't matter how much money a guy has. There are things guys don't like, and one of those is being nagged. Ash can tell he's not going to win this one, so maybe that makes him smarter than I thought.

"Alright. Just wait here."

Oh shit! For real? I have to see this. I have my phone in my other pocket, and I quickly dig it out because, uh, who the heck wouldn't want to get this recorded? The audio might not be as good as my recorder, still!

Meryl has her back to the top of the stairs, and Ash has walked off. I make a fast break for it, scrambling from the couch over to the side of the stairs where they curve. That should hide me from view, but I can still get a pretty good shot of this going down. I get out my rag to make it look like I'm dusting something, though what, I don't know because all that's around the impressive staircase with the dark iron banister and metal scrollwork is a bunch of air.

I very nearly lose my courage when I hear Ash's heavy steps coming back, but nope. That's not going to happen. This one is for my dad.

V meets engeance.

Yup, it's time for vengeance.

Ash comes back, a little black velvet box held out in front of him like it really does have some terrible voodoo curse stuff going on with it. Meryl actually gasps, and not a good sound either, while I find myself sucking in a silent breath. All of a sudden, my hand does something silly. It wavers, or maybe it's a giant tremor going through my arm, and Ash cracks the box.

The sound of the hinge opening sounds like Pandora's Box snapping open, and basically, all shit breaks loose as the sound scares the crap out of me. My hand wavers again, and my phone goes clattering to the floor. I have a big case on it, so it's unharmed, but the noise is violent. Meryl lets out a shriek and flails in surprise. Her hand hits the ring box, which sends it flying. The box goes bouncing down the stairs, hitting just about every step on its way down. Somehow, it comes to a stop right at the bottom, lid facing up, the ring sitting on its cushion just like a tiny little egg in the middle of a nest, miraculously spared from the kind of fall that should have cracked its shell and spilled out all its insides.

I think fast, snatching up my phone and tucking it away. I have my cleaning rag, and I clear my throat like I just got there and haven't been standing at the bottom of the steps the whole time, eavesdropping madly.

I snatch the box up and look up the stairs.

"Uh, I...Elisa? That's your name, right?" Ash leans over the top. He's all chiseled features, a shock of jet-black hair, and piercing blue eyes, which makes my insides do something very strange.

Including my brain. A brain blip. That's what it does. Because the box is open, and that ring with the ornate gold setting and big diamond in the middle surrounded by all those little diamonds is...I don't know. This is going to sound crazy, but it's like it calls to me with all its pretty, shiny diamond and gold glory. I don't think. Instead, I just react as one hand plucks it out while the other hand is already flexing, my fingers straightening. My brain just short circuits itself straight out, and there is nothing but pleasant and peaceful silence in my head.

However, it is abruptly shattered by this weird pounding, like drummers drumming, and then a scream like the wail of a thousand ghosts all joined in a ghostly choir at some bizarre church in my head, with chanters chanting, urges urging, and my blood surging. *Put it on. Put it on. Put it on.*

So, I do. I slip it straight onto my left hand, onto my ring finger.

And what do you know? It's a perfect fit.

2

ASH

Holy, epic, cursed shit. She put the ring on. Onto her finger. She's wearing the cursed soulmate ring!

"Elisa," I hear myself snap. My voice sounds a lot like my frayed nerves at the moment—raw and ready to go straight over the edge. "Take it off right now!"

"It's cursed!" Meryl screeches. "Get it off! Oh god, get it off before something happens to you."

I thought neither of us believed in it being cursed but listen to us now.

Elisa studies us from the bottom of the stairs, where she has this trance-like expression on her face. It's a pretty face, even with all the blankness going on. She doesn't smile or frown or react at all. Her eyes are an abnormal shade of... of...what the fuck? Are her eyes supposed to be that blue? They're like melting ice, the depths of the sea, and a strange aquamarine. They're also permanently fixed open, staring forward.

Meryl gasps from beside me. "Oh shit. She's in a trance. It's eating her soul. That ring really is cursed! Ash, we have to help her. Now!" Meryl takes off down the stairs, gripping the railing to keep from toppling on those crazy heels she has on. She must seriously like them because I've never seen her in anything else.

Why the hell am I thinking about heels when that ring might be devouring my maid's soul?

I race down the winding staircase after my fake fiancé to be, and we both stop when we reach Elisa, who hasn't moved and is still looking up at the top of the stairs. I can see her chest rising and falling. Thank god. But her eyes. I'm pretty damn sure her eyes are not supposed to be that color. Her full coral lips are parted ever so slightly in surprise. She has a pretty olive undertone to her skin, but two pink spots still make themselves known on her cheeks. With a heart-shaped face and an absolute riot of mahogany hair with rich copper highlights, she's quite pretty.

You know, if it wasn't for the fact that her eyes are doing this weird thing that makes her look like she could produce alien babies out of them from another dimension.

"She's not moving!" Meryl snaps her fingers in front of Elisa's face. "Oh my god, she's not...she's not responding. She's just frozen there."

Fear sinks itself like a bird of prey into my flesh, and goosebumps break out all over my skin. I'm wearing a t-shirt, and as per usual, my t-shirt and jeans are paint-stained since I was working on an art piece before Meryl got here. I didn't change because she knows I'm an artist and doesn't mind seeing me all paint-spattered. She always looks immaculate, but she has no expectations that I have to be the same way behind closed doors. Ours isn't a real relationship, so she technically has zero expectations from me at all. The only thing she wants is a nice smile and a fake front whenever other people are watching, which is pretty much whenever I exit the house.

Five minutes ago, the fake fiancé, fake wedding, fake marriage thing was my greatest concern.

But now, add my maid to the mix—dear lord, should I really use that word? Now *Elisa* has been turned into a statue with the bloody cursed ring on her bloody finger. Bloody fucking hell.

"Try and…and smack her!"

Meryl looks at me in horror. "I'm not going to smack her! What the heck is wrong with you? That would be assault."

"Not assault-style smack! Okay, yeah, maybe that's not good. Just…uh…grab her shoulders and try to shake her out of it."

"She's in a trance! What if I shake her and her neck snaps?"

"That probably won't happen."

"You shake her then!"

"If I shake her, it would be more forceful."

"Restrain yourself and do it."

With a sigh, I reach out toward Elisa's shoulders, but my hands pause in mid-air. "I can't do it." I drop them. "We should call an ambulance."

"And tell them what? About a cursed ring? They're not going to believe it. Or what if they do, and we get in serious shit? It would be bad. If people found out we're messing around with curses and stuff, they'll boycott the papers and magazines because they think it's bad luck."

"I think it would actually sell more. People love paranormal stuff."

"Not bad voodoo stuff like this!"

"Oh, I think you might be wrong there."

Meryl stamps one heel hard on the tiled stair. "Just shake her!"

"Why don't I just take the ring off?"

"O...oh." My future fake fiancé wraps her arms around her middle. She's scared. And for a good reason. This kind of stuff doesn't happen every day. Well, okay, it never happens. "Yeah, try and slide it off."

I can see that Meryl isn't going to be of any further help. She's a nice lady, and at thirty-four, she's only a year younger than me. We grew up in the same kind of environment, sort of. And we both went to Ivy League Schools. Our families both come from old money and then turned it into a mountain of new money in the same kind of arena. When I met her, we had a lot in common, and everyone wanted us to click. However, we just stayed business contacts and sort of friends until Meryl broached the idea of a fake wedding so everyone would stop asking when we'd get married and leave us alone to get on with our lives after the fact.

It made sense. It made a lot of sense. Meryl is smart, and she's more than just beautiful. She's stylish, witty, funny, and kind, but we have zero physical chemistry. I'm not it for her, and she's not it for me. Meryl is driven, and she's usually quite brave, but this cursed ring business has her shaken.

It even makes me quake a little in the boots I don't have on, as I'm more of a barefoot kind of guy when I'm painting. In order to make their point known, my toes flex on the cool tile and then curl. Because this is literally some toe-curling stuff right here.

"Ash? Are you going to—"

"Yes. Yes, I'm going to get it off." It sounds filthy, but neither of us makes a gutter-humored joke about it. It's not Meryl's style, and it's not mine either unless I'm with my brother and cousins. They're my best friends, and when we're together, things can get just a little bit crass. And by little, I mean a lot. As in, a butt-ton.

I reach out toward Elisa's hand. Her hand is outstretched

still, her fingers flexed, and she hasn't moved. She really is still frozen. I inch forward with my index finger, letting it lead the way, closer and closer.

"Arghhhhh," Meryl suddenly sighs, scaring the heck out of me.

I shiver violently but keep going. I close the distance and only hesitate once when I'm a few inches away. Then, I just go for it. I handled that stupid box just fine a few minutes ago, so I tell myself I can do this. The ring isn't going to zap me. It's supposed to lead me to my soulmate or some nonsense, which means good things, not bad. The bad things happen to people who put it on who are not my soulmate, clearly. Look at poor Elisa, frozen as still as a statue.

Thank god I didn't let Meryl have it. And good thing I made that pact with my cousins and brother. Curse or no curse, we are never falling in love. Not after the whole fiasco of a mess we witnessed our parents go through even though theirs were love marriages. But even if that hadn't happened, we probably still wouldn't have believed in love because we're modern individuals with lots of money and sense. And love is just kind of a ridiculous notion to believe in. Anyway, I'm going to fight this curse tooth, nail and all of that if I have to, that is if, by some very minuscule chance, it actually was real.

I grasp the ring and wait for it to obliterate me. Or Elisa. Or maybe incinerate the house, bring a UFO down through the roof, create some swirling black smoke and one hell of a pissed-off magician, or perhaps just some inky, nasty, deadly smoke. But nope. Nothing.

Except, when I try to pull the ring, which doesn't feel overly tight on Elisa's finger, it doesn't budge. I grasp it with all my fingers around her finger and tug. But nope, still nothing. I plant my feet firmly on the step and pull. Again, a whole lot of nothing.

Then, I pulled it even harder because, you know, the third time is the charm and everything. And what do you know, the ring finally budges. I can feel it. It slides a whole possible nanometer or whatever tiny measurement that's barely discernable, but it doesn't move more than that.

The effect, though, is just about instant. Elisa lets out a great big gasp, rips her hand from mine, and comes back to life. Her face switches from surprise to indignation and confusion. She flexes her hand—the hand with the ring—then stares Meryl and me down.

"What the heck is going on?"

"You...you put the ring on!" Meryl gasps. "And you were frozen in time. Like a statue. Right here on the step. We tried to get it off you because it seriously is cursed, but it wouldn't come off. Ash must have budged it a bit because...uh...you finally snapped out of it."

Elisa blinks at us and slowly looks down at the ring. "That's not...that's not possible. It's a perfect fit. It slid on easily. It should just come off..." She trails off, diverting her attention to the insidious bastard of a cursed object on her left hand. She curls the fingers of her right hand around it and tugs. Then, she tugs again. Her lips part. "That's weird."

"We have to get it off!" Meryl all but screams right into my ear. "Now!"

"Whoa..." Elisa backs up, putting her hands up to ward us off. "No way. Okay, this is my hand, my body. Whatever you're thinking..."

"Nothing like that," Meryl assures her. "I was thinking soap and water? Olive oil from the kitchen maybe? Some kind of jelly?"

"Ewwww. Um, okay. I...yeah. Let's try that, I guess. I'm

sorry. I...what the heck just happened? Did you say I was frozen?" Things are obviously starting to sink in because Elisa shudders. Her whole body moves with it, from her shoulders to her fingers, her middle, her legs, and her toes.

It's a very inappropriate moment to notice the curves my maid is sporting beneath a plain white t-shirt and a set of dark skinny jeans, but I'm not blind, and the shudder that just made her sway in an entirely provocative manner, thrusting out nice, full breasts and shaking curvy hips, didn't help.

I tear my eyes away fast and drop them down to her...to the ring. Yes, to the ring. "Don't worry, Elisa. We'll figure it out. There is no such thing as curses. I promise."

"Ha!" She yelps. "No such thing? Why was I just...frozen? You said I was frozen! I only remember putting it on. It's like...it's like it called to me. How did the box tumble down the steps and land right side up anyway with the ring perfectly intact inside? I heard this...well, it was like drums in my head or something. And my brain was pounding. It felt like...like...I don't know. The urge to put it on was *real*. I don't know why I did it. I just...I'm *sorry*." She looks forlorn for a second, but then she collects herself, inhaling sharply, and her eyes narrow. "Wait a minute. Did you just call me Elisa? Again?"

"That's your name, isn't it?"

She snorts. "Rich assholes never remember anyone's name."

"Excuse me?" Did she honestly just call me a rich asshole right to my face? The look of derision she shoots at me has some borderline super hostile tendencies going on underneath.

"It's not Elisa?" Meryl steps in. She asks kindly, and usually, women have this odd competitive thing going on with Meryl. I guess it has to do with her being really pretty. Women tend not to like other pretty women, but the maid whose name I apparently do not know because I'm a *rich asshole* actually calms down and gives Meryl a genuine smile.

"No. It's Ellis."

"Ellis is a guy's name," I protest. "Maybe that's why I thought it was Elisa."

"Ellis was the name my parents gave me. It was my mom's favorite, and she's no longer in this world, so that alone makes me proud to have it," EllisnotElisa snaps at me.

"Okaaaayyyyy," Meryl cuts in. She steps down and wraps an arm around my hostile, and probably now cursed, maid's shoulders. "Let's go into the kitchen and see if we can find some oil to get the ring off."

I watch them go, shaking my head. I start a mantra in my brain as I trail a safe distance behind. Safe as in safe from Ellis finding something to hurl at me or scowling me into oblivion.

I refuse to believe in curses because if curses are real and that ring won't come off Ellis' finger, what does that mean for me? For her? *For us*???

3

ELLIS

As I follow Meryl to a kitchen that looks nothing like the outside of the building, which is all brick and black wrought iron under every window, turrets, and other fancy things from a bygone era, I'm very aware I still have my recorder going in my back pocket. I really hope that whatever happened with the ring didn't short it out. If I lost the material from before I put the ring on, I'm going to lose my mind.

Honestly, my mind is on what I can do with that story, who I can sell it to, and the thousand ways I can ruin Ash Cromwell's life. It's not on the ring that has somehow crazy glued itself to my finger.

"Oh my god!" Meryl gasps after she turns to look at me.

We're standing by the kitchen counter, which is made of something weird like cement and crushed blue and green glass with a transparent resin covering it all, and there's a rack of pots above our head. I don't mind Meryl, but I swear, if she spotted my recorder and tries to take it, I'm not above beaning her with a frying pan. But no, not to kill her or anything, obviously. Just to stun her so I can run out the back door. Maybe I'd whack her in the leg to scare her and then take off. I eye the big wooden door not too far from us, just in case I have to make a fast break for it.

My car is parked out there, in the small drive carved out for this part of the house. I don't know why anyone so rich would want a house in the French Quarter. I mean, it's incredibly nice, but it's also highly touristy. If I were rich, I wouldn't want people up in my business, no matter how historic and tempting the property might be. Thankfully, this one isn't a funky color like most of them are. This one is brick, two stories, and is wider and longer than it is tall. It has rows and rows of windows on the first and second floors, each bracketed by a little wrought-iron decoration balcony-looking thing below it. The house is on a corner, and it takes up at least three lots going back. Also, it has a rooftop patio and garden.

Yeah, this place is freaking huge, and I hate cleaning. The maid gig is purely just for undercover purposes. If I had to clean this place all on my own, I think it would take me a hundred years just to work my way up to the rooftop.

"W...what?" I stammer. I grasp the weird countertop and stare at the glossy white cabinets so that it's not obvious I'm eyeing the pots above us.

"Your eyes."

Okay, that's not what I thought she was going for. "My eyes? My eyes what?"

"They were...on the stairs...they were, like, blue. Or green. I don't know. But they're not blue or green now."

"What color are they?" I'm a little bit creeped out, but I'm also losing my patience. Maybe they just wanted to scare me, or they're making this whole thing up as a great big joke, or maybe Ash knows I'm working as an undercover journalist, and he's making my life hell.

But no. It doesn't explain why I can't get the ring off when it's not a snug fit. It doesn't explain how Meryl and Ash got from the top of the stairs right to the bottom and were standing in front of me without me ever seeing them move. And it certainly doesn't explain why I *feel* like there's a chunk of my life missing, even if only a few minutes. I feel like I blinked—one heck of a long blink—and missed something in time. Something I can't get back.

"Amber. I think." Meryl leans a little closer, and she smells good. Like sweet sugar, cotton candy, or something sweet. Icing maybe? Anyway, I like it, whatever it is. "Brown with gold flecks?"

"That's my normal color."

"They're very pretty. I like them."

"Umm...thanks?"

Meryl shakes herself with a flutter of her blonde hair, and more of the delicious burnt sugar scent fills the air around her. "Right. Sorry. Oil."

I want to ask her where the heck Ash went. Not because I want him anywhere near me, tugging at the ring, staring me down, or getting my name wrong, but because I don't like that I can't see him. He might be plotting something.

Like what? How to cut my finger off with a pair of shears? He doesn't own a chainsaw or a lawnmower because he has people to do that for him—groom his little patch of backyard. Also, scissors wouldn't work, and the knives are in the kitchen. For the moment, it appears that I'm safe.

Unless there's an automatic garbage disposal under the kitchen sink.

As it is, I barely resist the urge to look over the big, hammered copper sink. It's the grandest sink I've ever seen, and it probably cost a fortune. I'll never forgive it for being so amazing if it grinds my finger off.

While I'm thinking rather graphic, bloody thoughts about my poor finger, Meryl finds a bottle of virgin olive oil. She holds it up and grins at me. "Okay, we'll just slather this on and wait a minute, and then it should slip right off. Oil always works for me. Over the years, I've had a few rings get stuck." She blushes almost instantly and clears her throat. "Um, I…yeah. But not on that finger, though."

I obediently hold out my hand over the countertop while she pours a profuse amount of oil. Then, she grabs a roll of paper towel and throws some onto the puddle on the cement top.

"These are pretty cool," she says as if she's never noticed any of the fixtures in the house. She's glancing at all the broken glass pieces in the cement. "And rather heavy looking. I wonder how they installed them."

"I'm not sure."

Her lips press together, and her eyes dance. "Right, sorry. We're in the middle of dealing with a creepy, cursed ring here, not talking about countertops and interior design."

"While we are…" I take in the glossy cabinets and drywall. "What do you think? It's kind of a shame all that nice brick was covered up."

"Indeed. Brick is a real thing in New York."

"It's probably a thing here too. Whoever chose this design should be shot."

"That would be me." Ash's deep voice—his very *unamused* voice—makes me jump, and drops of olive oil fling from my hand.

"Shit!" I put my hand over my chest, right where my heart is thundering. "Uh, sorry?"

He shakes his head, and his eyes lower to my hand. "Want to give it a try?"

"Okay." I grasp the ring. My fingers slip over all the little stones, and also the big one. Yikes, that's a *huge* diamond in there. Curse, my ass, because this ring is worth a fortune. Ash is probably worried about it, seeing as it's expensive and a family heirloom. He didn't even want to give it to Meryl. He was going to make her a cheap replica and probably ask for a cubic zirconia.

What? He's rich, but he's also a sneaky snake, just like the rest of his family. His grandmother bought out my dad's paper and promised not to close it. But then, she did just that.

I get a firm hold of the ring and tug. Nothing happens. Then, I twist it. Hard. Still nothing.

"For the love of..." Ash cuts himself off and grabs the dish soap from the back of the sink. It's some fancy, biodegradable, earth-friendly kind.

He squirts a liberal amount of it all over my finger, and before I can protest, he touches me. Like, my finger, with his hand. His big, tapered, strong, male fingers wrap around mine and start rubbing back and forth over the ring. Heat pools in my finger and shoots right up my arm. It also unfurls between my legs in the most shameful, annoying way.

What the hell, traitor vagina? You're getting all bent out of shape for Ash freaking Cromwell?

He rubs, and rubs, and then tugs at it. Trust me when I say it's not as sexy as it sounds. Or is it? My body, annoyingly enough, is flooded with another wave of heat and a fresh wave of something else that I don't care to define. My nipples are painfully erect, but thank goodness my sports bra is nice and tight and has cups that won't let them poke through. I hope.

Unfortunately, the ring doesn't budge.

"Ice?" Meryl suggests. She runs to the huge, double-door

fridge, which is a matte black because I guess that's stylish and expensive, and pulls out a bag of frozen peas. "Peas?" She raises a brow at Ash. "You eat peas?"

"I like peas," Ash huffs. "Is that a crime?" He takes the peas from Meryl, bends his dark head with all his long, lovely, thick hair, and sets the bag on top of my hand.

What the heck! Am I seriously focusing on his hair? Do I really want to run my hands through it to see just how soft and silky it is? Does rich person hair feel different from regular person hair? And why is there no gray? Does he see a stylist or a barber or whatever for more than just a cut?

When I can't feel my hand, I start to protest. Ash grabs the bag of peas, tosses them aside carelessly, and starts to work at the ring again. He twists, tugs, and tugs some more. He also rubs it back and forth before twisting it again, which still sounds just wrong. However, it's still a big no-go.

"Hey, I don't mean to be a huge, uh, pain here, but I'm going to miss my flight if I don't leave now," Meryl announces as Ash steps back.

He lets out a sigh that says he's quite frustrated and annoyed. His big, broad shoulders heave up and down, and his paint-stained t-shirt tightens along his midsection. My gaze lowers to check out Ash's ass, and maybe I should get a career as a psychic because I called him Ash Asswell, at least to myself, long before I ever took notice of his behind, and just...wow! It's definitely an ass, and it's definitely *well.* My nipples grow so stiff and tight that they're at risk of cutting glass, let alone fabric. To get a hold of myself, I grip the counter harder with the hand that isn't all covered in oil and soapy goo.

"That's alright," Ash says, clearly moderating his tone to only let out what he wants us to hear. None of his frustration seeps through. "I'll call you and give you an update later."

"Okay. Good luck." As she heads out of the kitchen, Meryl gives me a sympathetic look that wins her major nice points in my book.

When we're alone, Ash faces me, and his nice, bronzed complexion starts to turn into a not-so-nice scarlet. I can hear him grinding his teeth, and it's nasty. It's like he's eating gritty sand. Or kitty litter. Ha! It would serve him right to get a few cat biscuits to munch with it.

"Please stop that. It's not going to help get this freaking cursed ring off my finger."

"This is your fault." Ash stabs a finger at me. His crazy blue eyes get even bluer. And a little crazier.

"My fault?" I gasp. "How is this my fault? It was begging me to put it on! There were drums in my head. Freaking. Drums. It was calling to me, screaming at me, and it was so weird. It was like there was someone else in my body that made me do it."

Those sky blues of Ash's go skyward as he rolls them. "Seriously? Don't start with that now. If you're faking this, you're doing an excellent job, but you don't have to sell it anymore. Whatever you want, just name your price, and it's yours."

My whole body goes cold, and it feels like all the blood has drained out of me and disappeared, leaving me a shriveled-up prune of a mess. "Uh, what do you mean by name your price? You think... you think I'm faking this to blackmail you?" *If only you knew...* I ignore the sinister sound of my inner voice and instead focus on the righteous indignation working its way up from my toes to my throat. "You've tried to pull the ring off. It doesn't look tight, but it won't budge. Am I faking that? Maybe you're the one faking it. If that's the case, maybe you should name your price."

Ash's nostrils flare, and a storm gathers in his eyes. I kind of like it, despite myself. Ash rubs his hands on his faded, paint-stained jeans, and when I lower my gaze, I realize he's barefoot. How could I have missed that? The sight of his bare toes is strangely alluring.

What the actual hell is going on? This must be the curse. Even if it's not, I'm blaming it anyway.

"Until the ring comes off, you are staying here."

"Staying here?" I gasp. "You can't hold me a prisoner!"

"You're not a prisoner. But the ring is worth a lot of money, and if you walk out of here, I'm calling the cops. If you want to end up at the cop shop and have them try to remove it, just go ahead. Go right on out. But don't test me on it because I *will* call them."

"I think calling a jeweler or a paramedic would make more sense."

At my words, Ash's face brightens. "That's a great idea. I'll call a jeweler. They have tools to cut it off."

"No!" I yelp so hard that we both jump. "I...what if... what if cutting into the ring releases more curses? Something terrible? I don't think that's a good idea. Plus, I heard it really hurts and can cause damage to the skin and finger and hand."

Ash actually seems to soften, which shocks me. I didn't realize any of the Cromwellian buttholes were truly capable of human emotion. "Fine. I'll give you until tomorrow morning. If you can't get it off by then, I'm calling a jeweler. You can stay in the spare room upstairs, and since you clean here, you probably know where it is."

"Where...are you...you're going to be here?"

"Yes, I am. I'll be in my studio, finishing up the painting

I'm working on. You have until tomorrow morning! You understand, *Elisa*?"

Oh, so that's how you want to play this. Well, I can play along too, Ash Asswell.

"Yeah," I mutter. "I get it." But then, because I'm a journalist, and I have a bit of a big mouth and a problem with not voicing my thoughts, and also because I don't want to be haunted by images of my finger getting detached from my body all night, I have to blurt, "What if it doesn't work? The jeweler, I mean? What if he can't get it off? Or cut through it?"

Ash grins that evil, signature, Cromwellian grin. "Well, let's hope it doesn't come to that."

Yes, let's hope indeed. Because I'm rather partial to my finger, thank you very freaking much. "Are you a psycho?"

"Excuse me?"

"If I'm going to spend the night here, I need to know you're not a psycho." I glance down at the ring. "Wait, yeah, *you're totally a psycho.*"

"The spare bedroom has a lock on the door, just like most of the rooms here. You have nothing to worry about."

"Oh, I see." I lift my eyes to the ceiling. The pot rack is still up there. Death by frying pan is so appealing right now, but I honestly don't want to go out as the murdering kind. "Other than the whole ring and curse thing, then yup, absolutely nothing at all to worry about."

"Exactly." Ash's tone has a brutal finality, and he leaves me there with a bunch of goo coating my hand to figure out how to fix this all on my own.

4

ASH

That cursed ring—damn it, I don't believe in curses—that *ring* couldn't have landed on the finger of a sassier, more annoying, more infuriating woman.

Overnight, I decided that my immediate life has boiled down to one thing and one thing only, which is detaching the ring from Ellis' finger and firing her, so I never have to see her again. I couldn't get her strange eyes—those weird sea-colored orbs *or* the amber-hued ones—out of my mind all night. I had creepy dreams. Creepy ones that turned taboo. Dreams about Ellis standing before me, wearing only the ring and a taunting smile, and holy shit, I'll cut it off right there. I have no control over my dreams. I know that. But still.

Normally, I love getting up early when things are still quiet and gray, and I usually opt for a good workout. But not this morning. This morning, I'm bleary and unfocused, and I desperately need to get my head into the game. Nothing makes that clearer than when I stumble into the kitchen for a cup of coffee to try and beat back the sensation of utter exhaustion, and I find Ellis down there already hard at work with the jug of dish soap and the olive oil again. I become instantly surly for no reason at all that I can explain.

Well, other than the fact that my maid, who clearly has it in for me, has a cursed family heirloom stuck to her body, and the heirloom is supposed to belong to my soulmate and my soulmate alone.

And she's definitely not it!

But I do have to admit, soulmate or not, Ellis in her immaculate clothing from the day before, with her wild dark hair mussed and hanging halfway down her back in a free fall of rich velvet lushness, and her amber eyes wide and hopeful, reminds me just a little bit too much of the strange dreams I had last night. The reminder makes me flush, and I don't flush or fluster.

Usually.

Also, I realize her clothing isn't rumpled, which means she probably didn't sleep in her jeans or t-shirt. Was she birthday suiting it between the sheets? Naked? No! No, I can't go there. The last thing I need is this annoying semi to change into an even more annoying, raging hard-on.

I scramble for a coffee cup, turning my body away from her so she can't see that I'm suddenly rock hard in my jeans. She made coffee, I notice. When I angle around just a little, I can see that there's an empty cup on the counter not too far away. It's seven in the morning. What time does this girl get up?

I help myself to a cup of coffee, ignoring the fact that what I really want is a cup of *her*. Wait, no! No, what I technically want is the ring off her finger and her out my front door, kitchen door, back door, or rooftop door. Just any door will do. Although perhaps not the rooftop door. There aren't any stairs leading down from there, so the descent would be somewhat questionable, and I don't want to get sued on top of everything.

"Good morning," she said. "Did you sleep well in this huge, creaky, and strange house? How's the ring going? Do you feel creepily cursed? Why did your eyes change color the day before? How's that going for you? Is your health okay, or has a demon taken over your body?"

I whirl so fast that my coffee gurgles in my mug, nearly tossing itself over the rim and onto the floor. I find Ellis staring me down, and she's not smiling. Her entire hand is coated in soap and oil on top of a blanket of paper towels on the island countertop.

"I highly doubt any worse demon could inhabit your body other than what is already in there."

"What's that supposed to mean?" she huffs. "I didn't do this on purpose!"

"Didn't you?" I raise an eyebrow.

"Even if I did, it's not my fault the bloody thing won't come off!"

"We're not going through this again."

Ellis grabs the olive oil, turns it upside down, and dumps it all over the place. I let out a grumpy-sounding grunt at the fact that it's now everywhere. "If it doesn't come off, I thought we could try something else. Something other than cutting it off because I'm still not sure that's the best option."

"We could cut your finger off to save the ring," I supplied helpfully. And dryly.

Ellis' eyes get huge, but then I guess she figures out from my tone that I'm not serious, and she relaxes a little. She looks great, everything considered. She has zero bags under her eyes, and even in just a regular t-shirt and jeans with her hair in a pretty, wild mane, she's gorgeous. Even far more beautiful than Meryl. At least, I think so. But maybe it's just my dick talking, and I learned a long time ago not to listen to that appendage's advice.

"I was thinking more like go to a psychic or someone who reads tarot cards and get them to give us some advice."

"Right. Get some touristy fraud-y type of person to tell us how to remove a cursed ring."

"Not them!" Ellis gives me that overly patient kind of look that frazzled mothers often give their children when they are two seconds away from losing their control and raising their voice, causing shit to get hairy. "The cards! Or like the ball or whatever they use."

"Oh, right. Here we go." I can't even have this conversation, so I gulp back some of the coffee and very nearly spit it right back out. "Holy Hannah, what did you do to make this so strong?"

She lifts one pretty little shoulder and shrugs. "I don't know. I just put in what I always put in. Twelve scoops."

"Twelve?! You put twelve scoops of coffee in to make a pot?"

She stares at me blankly. "If it's not strong, then why bother?"

God. No wonder she looks so perky. No, not perky, but awake or chipper. And also eye bag-less.

"Anyway," she goes on before adding more oil to her hand. "I guess if the ring really is cursed, the cards would know. Like it would turn over all the scary cards for me."

"I think you've inhaled too much New Orleans tourist mumbo-jumbo."

Her lips twitch, and I'm so very delighted that I could be a source of amusement at this time. "Do people still use that word? Mumbo-jumbo? I haven't heard it in, like, I don't know. Ever. Because it hasn't been a thing since before I was born."

"I'm not that much older than you, so don't look at me like that."

"Oh, right. Yeah, twelve years isn't much at all. What's a decade or two here and there?"

"That explains it." I take another long pull of coffee, sucking it back and swallowing before the butt load of bitter can hit me.

"Explains what?"

"Explains why you buy into garbage like that. You haven't had time to get jaded."

"Says the man who professes not to believe in curses but so obviously does."

This time I set my mug down so hard that the coffee does slosh over the rim. "Pull it off and leave. Please. I'll give you three months of severance pay. Just don't come back because this is truly the last thing I need."

"If you're so worried about falling in love or finding a soulmate, why didn't you just destroy the ring? You know, toss it in a fiery pit? Isn't there a movie about that? Oh right. There are plenty of movies and a whole bunch of books about cursed items."

"I couldn't just destroy it. What's wrong with you? The ring belonged to my great-great-grandma, and it would kill my granny. Thanks, but no thanks on giving one of my favorite people a heart attack."

Ellis looks surprised at my words, but her voice is even more bitter than the disgusting coffee she brewed up, reminding me that apparently, she doesn't like me very much, which isn't a first for me, though people generally do like me. They also like my granny, and they loved my grandpa when he was still alive. Not only that, they loved my dad and uncle before both of them peaced out to live a life devoid of children and responsibilities. People love my mom and aunt as well, and generally, my brother and cousins are also well-liked. Since I'm an artist, people see me as pretty harmless, plus, who doesn't like art?

"You love your granny? Really? That's sweet."

"You make it sound like a crime."

"Nope. Don't know why you think that."

I'm about to get into the fact that she's currently staring razor-sharp daggers at me, but then she lifts her hand—strings of oil and soap trailing down to the counter—grasps the ring, and pulls. She pulls so hard that she turns red in the face, and I can see the muscles in her arms bulging. She isn't faking it.

"Fuck!" she screams. "Fuck, fuck, fuck, fuccccckkkkkkk! Motherfucking fucker of a ring!"

She's not faking the sailor's mouth either.

"Whoa. Hey. Calm down."

Ellis spins on me, her eyes flashing so bright that it's like walking through the jungle and running into one of those amber-eyed cats intent on eating you up. "Calm down?! Calm down?! You're the one talking about cutting off my freaking finger or this cursed thing to bits, which is also off my finger. I'm the one with it stuck on, and you're telling me to *calm down*?!"

Sensing an explosion is imminent, I do the first sensible thing I can think of to deflect. "Uh, the cards. Yes, you're right. Let's go get a tarot card reading done."

Ellis reacts like I just slapped her, and she freezes. "Are you serious?"

"Yeah, sure. Let's go and see if anyone can tell us if the ring truly is cursed, then we'll talk about cutting into it. You might be right. I don't want to risk it. Uh, but where are we supposed to find someone to do the reading?"

She barks out a laugh. "Um, you live in the French Quarter, so just walk down the street. And for a guy who doesn't believe in all the NOLA, touristy, *mumbo-jumbo*, you sure picked a house right in the middle of it."

"My family is from here, and I wanted to be in the historical heart of the city. I'll have you know I'm actually an art and history major."

I don't know if I'm trying to impress Ellis with that information, but I fail miserably because she tosses her hair over her shoulder with a hard flick of her neck and gives me what my grandpa liked to call the stink eye. She's good at it too. I wither on the spot.

"Yes, you went to college and got a double major because your family has money coming out the wazoo, and you can afford to get useless degrees. Also, you're only an artist because of your family connections. You're...you're like those people who just splash paint on a canvas, call it art, and then sell it for crazy amounts of money. If I tried that, it would end up sitting in a pile at a garage sale, a *picked-over* garage sale, because that's all it would be good for."

Considering what we're dealing with, I'd say tensions are running high. I've heard the jab about how to make art a thousand times, so I'm going to be the better person and take the high road here. I point at Ellis' nasty hand. "You might want to clean that up before we go."

She gives me another stinker of a stink eye and turns toward the sink behind her. "Whaaaaaaaa!" She lets out a screech that could raise the hairs on the back of Satan's neck himself as she starts flailing wildly. I realize she's slipped on something, probably spilled oil on the floor, and I find myself moving.

I'm a fairly athletic guy. I work out pretty hard still, and my reaction time is excellent, which is lucky for Ellis. Because as she's going down, I rush over, grasp her arm, and steady her. But then she flails with the other hand, hits a messy puddle of oil on the counter again, and screeches. I steady her further—meaning I keep her from killing herself with oil and dish soap—by pulling her tight against my chest and wrapping my arms around her.

I bend my head to reassure her that she's fine, but instead, I find myself closing my eyes, and suddenly, I'm kissing her.

Not an innocent peck on the lips, either. No. This is a full, open-mouthed, hungry, raw type of kiss, lips devouring lips. Her mouth is warm and surprisingly welcoming. I wouldn't say mine is demanding, but I'm persistent, and she's not making noises of protest. My brain hasn't snapped into its normal function where it tells me I shouldn't do this, so I keep doing it. I graze my teeth over Ellis' bottom lip. She whimpers, and as her lips part, I sweep my tongue through the seam, not like an invasion, but gently.

Ellis' hands come up, but she doesn't shove me away. Instead, she tangles them around my neck and lets me coax her tongue into a warm caress with mine. I'm about to go for another when something wet and slithery slides down my neck.

I tear away, frantically batting at whatever just crawled onto me before I realize it's oil—oil and soap from Ellis' hand.

She turns quickly, hiding her face from me, and heads for the sink. She washes her hands while I get a paper towel and start cleaning up the mess. I go for my neck first, then tackle the countertop and floor. I don't want any more mishaps, missteps, or catching Ellis with my lips, saving her from falling with my mouth, or ensuring she's okay with my tongue.

She whips around as I'm cleaning up the last bit of oil off

the countertop. I expect to find total disgust there, anger bordering on rage, a lecture waiting to happen, maybe even malice—hell, I hardly know her, but she seems tough—but instead, I only find confusion.

"Can we please not talk about that?"

"Right. Yes, of course. I'm—"

"No. I don't want to go there. Don't say sorry because it never happened, and it will never happen again, so there is nothing to apologize for."

I throw the wad of oily paper towels into the trash beneath the sink. I can feel Ellis' stare burning through my back the whole time, and when I turn, I have something logical to say, but something highly illogical comes out instead. "Maybe it was the ring."

"What?" she yelps.

"It could have been. It could be making us do strange things."

"Oh, right. Yeah, of course. It's the curse in full motion." A little bit of red starts crawling up her neck, just above the neckline of her t-shirt. "Can we just go, please? I want to get this thing off."

"Yes, alright." *Am I seriously doing this?*

What I should be doing is calling my brother and cousins and warning them that this curse we all made a pact to ignore might be real. Then, I should head over to my granny's house and give her a piece of my mind for daring to meddle in our lives like this. She should know better than anyone that happily ever after is not a thing. All we ever really have is right now ever after. Everything else is just a bunch of bullshit because people suck, and they never get it right. She watched her two sons destroy their marriage and abandon their family, and she still dared to give us this haunted crap. My god, she has lady balls the size of grapefruits.

"Ash?" Ellis stops at the kitchen door, which I don't think I've ever used before.

"What?" Her eyes are so big and frightened and pleading that it makes something in my chest get a little hairy. And no, it's not chest hair. I take care of that with my razor, thank you very much.

"Please don't mention the curse. If it's real, let it not come for us."

I lower my gaze to the blasted ring stuck on Ellis' long, finely shaped finger on her sweet, delicate little hand. "Oh, I think it already has."

5

ELLIS

"What about this one?" I stop in front of an admittedly touristy-looking place.

The shop is tiny with a striped awning over a window that has bold gold letters painted on the glass, announcing tarot and palm readings. I don't wait for a response. I move up to the glass door, fling it open, and charge ahead. If I left it up to Mr. Asswell, I know he'd have us walking around all day, and honestly, I'm kind of in a hurry for someone to reassure me that everything is going to be okay.

Even if it's all nonsense.

The smell of incense is so thick that it wraps around me like a coat the second I step foot inside. The little building has brick walls—at least someone knows better than to cover them up—and shelves lined with all sorts of items such as books on tarot, palmistry, self-help, and more. There are long tables underneath the shelves with rows and rows of crystals, a stand of jewelry, and incense you can purchase.

I kind of like the one the shop owner chose as it smells like cloves and cinnamon. Just thinking about her seems to summon her. She's a tiny old woman with a shock of long bright pink hair who exits the back through a beaded curtain.

"Good morning," she says happily. "I'm Ginny. Can I help you find anything?"

"I...yes. I...I mean we...we would like to have our cards read."

Ash is still standing in the doorway, blocking a good deal of sunlight from coming through the glass door with his very fine...I mean, no. Not very fine body. More like his hulking, sulky form, especially since he has a perma-frown going on. However, my ovaries take note that he also has a heck of a lot of nice things going on, too, especially when wearing a tight black t-shirt and dark jeans that aren't paint-stained. Although, I like the paint-stained get-up too. I think he could wear anything and look good.

But it would be better if he wore nothing at all. Boo-yeah! My evil inner voice chimes in. My lady bits all seem to be in cahoots, and my nipples, va-jay, and ovaries all leap to attention. *Too bad he ruins it by barking orders and being surly, broody, and related to a bunch of newspaper-buying, promise-breaking soul crushers.* Regardless, my lady bits don't mind. In fact, they don't wither at all.

So, it means I have to face Ginny with a blush staining my face and a heck of a lot of fire swirling through my insides.

If she notices, she doesn't let on. "Certainly. I can do that for you right now if you want to follow me to the back." When Ginny moves out from behind the counter, I can see she's quite petite, probably somewhere around seventy, and is dressed in a long skirt, a peasant blouse, and a shawl wrapped around her waist. She paired her outfit with heavy silver earrings and a heavy turquoise necklace.

"Just a minute," Ash calls out as he stalks over and grabs

my arm. He steers me toward the door while I try to get over the fact that he's touching me. I mean, just my arm, but my nipples don't care. They're in overdrive, and my lady cave is sure to follow any minute. I swallow thickly, tamping down the hot wave of desire sweeping through me while I rip my arm away from him.

"What are you doing?" I hiss. "Who said you could touch me?" *Who said you couldn't? Wa-zing!* I ignore my inner cavewoman and paste on a snarl. "You said we should get a reading, so we're here. We're doing this."

"She's dressed like a fortune-teller, and she's burning enough incense to make a person high. There's also mood music playing." I notice he's right. Soothing sounds of nature pump over some hidden speakers somewhere. "This is all fake."

"So what? Every place looks like this. You think if they had some dank cave in which you had to enter, and it smelled all dank and foul, and there was a big simmering cauldron in the middle, then people would have more fun because it looks more authentic?"

"Yes. Honestly, I do."

"Sorry to inform you, but caves are in short supply, so we're staying here. And we're doing it. Besides, she seems super nice, and you're acting rude."

Ash takes a step back like I just physically smacked him. "Rude?" he scoffs. "You're the one who put on an engagement ring meant for someone else. And for the past day, you have done nothing but stereotyped my family using negative connotations, accused me of being a rich asshole, mocked my education, and said my art is in no way, shape, or form real art, and *I'm* the one being rude?"

My hands fly to my hips in a super bossy defensive mode. "First of all, you know why I put the ring on. It's because of all the bad voodoo voices and impulses that go along with the curse, which is solidly your fault. Second, you *are* rich, and you *are* an asshole. I have irrefutable proof of that. Also, I never mocked your education. I just said your degrees were useless because they are. And your art? Come on. It's just a bunch of paint splotches on a canvas. That doesn't pass as art in my books."

"You know what the main flaw in your argument is?"

"No." I roll my eyes hard enough to turn them inside out. "But I'm sure you're going to enlighten me with all your dazzling, enlightening, straight from the enlightenment era tricks."

"It's based on your opinion, not on real logic."

"My opinion *is* logic-based, so it's not a flaw."

Ash's lips thin out, his eyes thin out, and his nostrils thin out. Everything becomes thin and infuriated, but he has a good leash on his temper. And then, suddenly, he surprises me because his features return to their normal handsome state—*for the love of cream cheese, why do thoughts about Ash's physique keep popping into my head*—and he speaks calmly. With too much logic. Damn him.

"Alright, after we're done here, we'll see how logical it is. I'll point out to you all the uses for my degrees, and I'll make you a list of all the good things my family has done for this city. I really do resent you calling my granny, brother, and cousins assholes without even knowing them. And me too, for that matter. You don't know me either. Yes, I've been short about the ring, but it's not every day a person has to try and undo a legit curse, so I apologize that I've been a teeny, tiny, *littleeeee* bit *stressed*. But it doesn't make me an asshole. And if you think you can make better art, then by all means. I'll open up my studio when we get back to the house, and you can have at it."

"Right. Insert a hashtag here like they do on social media. Hashtag provemewrong. Hashtag reallyanasshole."

"You're ridiculous." Ash brings both hands up and rubs them from his forehead down to his chiseled jawline in utter exasperation. I wonder how many other people can make him do that.

"And you're just...just...well, you gave me this curse, and that about sums it all up perfectly. Hashtag fuckingcursed."

"Okay, I'm ready for you now. Who wants to go first?" Ginny interjects in the sweetest, firmest old lady—*I've had just about enough nonsense from you two today, and we haven't even started flipping these cards yet*—tone.

I turn and find her standing right beside us. By the door. I have no idea how she came from the back and walked up to us so silently. *Arggh!* The authentic creepiness just dialed itself way the heck up.

I think fast and point frantically at Ash. "He does."

He thinks fast and points frantically at me. "She does."

We speak and point at the same time. I want to stick out my tongue, but I'm afraid the ring might make my face freeze that way, just like my mom always threatened when I was young. I mean, it's cursed, and it made Ash Cromwell kiss me in his kitchen. It could make anything happen.

That kiss. No, I am not thinking about that kiss. No freaking way. That kiss, as far as I'm concerned, never happened. Ever. Never. What kiss? Right, the one from never.

"Just follow me," Ginny says sweetly. She moves off fast and silently, leaving us to work it out between ourselves.

"This was your idea," Ash says, so close that I can feel his breath on my neck—warm, minty, and sumptuous. It causes a strange vibration to rattle its way through me. "You should go first. After all, you're the one with the ring on."

"Fine. If you're too scared to get in that seat and let the fake lady do a fake reading, then I'll lady-up and show you that you have nothing to fear."

Ash is too smart to be goaded, so I guess he gets a point for that one. "Alright." He grins innocently at me. "Go for it."

I have no choice but to head to the back. It looks very much like the front, but with more tapestries hanging all over the walls and from the roof, giving it a cavernous, magical kind of look all on its own. The nature sounds are playing back here too, and the incense is so thick that it almost looks like clouds. The table is a small round one with two seats, one on either side. It's covered with a rich blue tapestry with gold embroidery along the edges, and it spans out in a pattern to the middle.

"What kind of a spread would you like?" Ginny sits down and waits for me to do the same. I slowly sink into the chair. It's a hard wooden one with a black leather seat. It's also antique and kind of uncomfortable, but maybe that's just my rigid-ass posture at the moment.

"Ummm..." Is it wrong that all I can think of for spreads is spread eagle? Yes! Yes, that is very, very wrong.

"Or tell me what you want to accomplish with the reading."

I practically feel Ash tense behind me. He's standing just a few paces back from the chair, looming over the table like a big, dark, sexy shadow. *Curse you cursed ring!* I swear it's putting these thoughts in my head. The curse has clearly spread from my mind down to my lady bits because that would explain an awful lot. Right, anyway, I can't just blurt out a big speech about this ring and why it won't come off my finger.

"Uh, I have a bit of a situation. I want to know what I should do and how it will turn out."

Ginny smiles at me. Goodness, she's so cute. Despite her advanced years, she doesn't have that many wrinkles, and her eyes are the deepest green I have ever seen. She also has a heart-shaped face that makes her look entirely youthful.

"The four-card spread would probably be best."

"Uh, alright. Sure. Yes, please." I realize I'm nervous, so I snap my mouth shut.

I watch Ginny take out her deck from a wooden chest on a side table. She treats it reverently, and it makes my breath catch. She shuffles it, glances at me, and then lays out four cards side by side on the table. I hold my breath until she sets the deck aside and looks at me.

"Are you ready?"

I want to say something along the lines of "No, I'm suddenly not," and literally run out of the shop, but that's not an option. For one, Ash would never let me live it down, and I can't stand him thinking I'm not brave enough to sit through my own freaking medicine. Or whatever. I was the one who suggested this, so I have to go through with it, massive waves of anxiety aside.

All I can do is nod, but Ginny smiles at me and reaches for the first card. I'm pretty sure she's one of those more positive people who interprets the cards in a favorable light. At least, I freaking hope so. If doom and gloom and finger cutting are in my future, I'd rather not have them written in stone. Or cards.

"Okay, so this first card represents the situation you're in, or the problem, or the question. Whatever you have in mind," Ginny starts. Her gnarled fingers hover over the first card, and when she turns it, I let out a breath. I know nothing about this, but she doesn't gasp or moan, so I figure it must be okay. "The two of cups. Interesting. The card is facing upright, which means balance. A good match. It doesn't always have to be romantic, but in your case..." Ginny's eyes don't even flick to Ash. I bet she has a lot of couples coming in here, or perhaps starstruck young women. I know she's probably reading me more than the card, telling me what she thinks I want to hear.

I want to laugh and tell her that I'm not here for romance. I'm here because I need to learn about a curse, but I keep that to myself. I suppose what she said could also relate to whatever problem, situation, or thing she said I have, except I don't like the answer. I guess it could even relate to the curse since the curse is supposed to be about love and soulmates and all that.

Ash stays totally silent and still behind me. I don't turn to look at him as I'm afraid to see his face.

"Should I continue?" Ginny asks patiently.

"Y...yes." I nod. "Yes, please."

Ginny turns over the next card. "The Ace of wands. Aces are powerful cards. They always symbolize something fresh. A new start, or as some people like to say, a rebirth. You've come to a place which allows you to cut ties with your old life and ways of thinking about things."

"Like I've seen the light," I put in dryly because nope, this is not going in a good direction.

Ginny smiles at me. "Yes. Exactly."

She flips the next card before I'm truly ready. "The seven of wands. This one is facing the wrong direction."

I swallow hard. Here comes the doom and gloom. "Is that bad?"

"No." Ginny beams at me. "Not at all. Seven is a good number. It indicates bravery, courage, and a decision to be made, even if it's hard and you don't know what path to take."

"Oh." I take a breath. Ash still hasn't said anything.

"One more. Here we go." Ginny turns over the last card. "The Hermit. Well, that's exactly what I was expecting." She chuckles, and I'm starting to think she's legit because she really did look like she was expecting it. "In this situation, I would say The Hermit means there is a guide waiting to help you on your way. But it can also be related to some deep soul searching."

All I can do is sit there frozen. That was so not what I was expecting. There were no scary cards—nothing indicating that the curse is bad. Also, there's nothing that tells me how to get this ring off my finger. Is there? By all accounts, those cards are telling me to keep it on. That if I can just get used to the idea and roll with the cursed punches, maybe I'm in for a pleasant surprise.

Ummm, we're talking about Ash Cromwell here. Destroyer of hopes and dreams. At least, his family is. And their business. He's the one I want to get revenge on, not end up spending time with. Especially not as my freaking soulmate.

"Okayyyyy." I leap up all happy and enthused, when deep inside, I'm freaking out even more. I vacate the seat and point to it. Ash looks...well...ashen. He's strangely pale, and now it looks like he doesn't want to sit. I stare at the seat until he finally moves and slips into it without so much as a creak, which is amazing because he's a big guy, and the chair doesn't look so sturdy.

Ginny gathers up the cards, slips them back into the deck, and shuffles again. "Same spread?"

Ash nods. What's good for the goose is good for the freaking gander, I guess. Yes, I just went there. Old-school clichés can be a wonderful thing.

Ginny lays out the cards, and the first one she turns over is The Magician. "Hmm," Ginny says. That's it. Just hmmm. Ash seems to draw into himself, bracing himself for something, and I find myself doing the same. "This can be very complex," Ginny sighs. "The universe is a big place, with many things we don't understand. There are so many options available to us if we just reach for them. Sometimes, how we view life isn't actually the way it is at all."

Ash says nothing, but inside, I'm mentally fist-bumping Ginny. If Ash thinks he's not a rich asshole, maybe now he'll change his tune. It could be his new awakening—a sort of enlightenment I'm going to give him when I get the ring off and go back to work. My recorder captured everything. He is totally going down.

But that would mean taking Meryl down with him, and I kind of like her.

I ignore the stab of guilt, the reading I had just completed, and what it could mean. Instead, I focus on steeling myself for what I have to do. All those cards could also have meant I have a big decision coming that I have to follow through with, and it will change the course of my life. As in, sell the story, or publish it. Maybe catch a few breaks and get Dad and me out of this rut. The happier relationship might not have meant love. It could have meant family. My dad, not Ash. *So there, curse. Eat it.*

The next card Ginny turns over is The Wheel of Fortune. Which is kind of funny, just because I associate it with TV and cash prizes, but anyway...

Ginny lets out a thin-sounding gasp, and I'm instantly drawn to attention. "Something has come into your life which you feel you have almost no control over, but this force has probably been there for a while. You've been grappling with it, trying to make the right decision on how to grow and change."

"What if I want to stop whatever is happening?" Ash

grinds out. He doesn't say it's the curse, which I'm thankful for.

Ginny looks at him hard. I bet she's a tough little old lady when she wants to be. "It's too late. You can't take it back, and I mean that in the best way. You shouldn't want to take it back. Just because the unexpected happens doesn't mean it's a bad thing. Sometimes, these things come about to show us a better way. I don't use words like fate, but if I were to drop the F-word, I would do it here."

"Fate?" Ash stares incredulously. "No. I don't believe in that."

Ginny just shrugs and turns over the next card. The Lovers. Of course, it's The Lovers. Before she can say anything, Ash leaps out of the chair. It skids backward and bumps into me, which keeps it from flying right over. I let out a grunt while Ash huffs. That's the last sound he makes before he storms out from the back. I hear the bell at the front door dingle merrily a few seconds later.

"Ummm...." I bite down on my bottom lip, fighting down shock and embarrassment. "I'm really sorry. We're, uh, that is...this is a hard time right now. For both of us."

Ginny nods. "Don't worry, honey. It's not the first time someone's got up and walked out during a reading."

"I'm still sorry. It's just rude."

"It's okay. Sometimes, people aren't ready to hear what the cards have to say."

I want to ask Ginny to tell me what it means. I want to ask her to turn over the next card, but I kind of already know she'll refuse. I do have to ask, though. "Is it weird that all those cards are like...not the suits cards I had?"

"It's unusual, yes," Ginny responds. "But not unheard of. The Major Arcana, they're called. And this card, just so you know, is frequently quite misunderstood. It often just means a bringing together of two things. Two different forces. A lot of the time, it can be internal."

"Conflict resolution?"

"Exactly."

"Ugh," I sigh. "I think he'll be relieved and hopefully feel pretty stupid about just ghosting you on that score."

"It's alright."

I have my purse slung over my shoulder, so I grab it and say, "Here. Let me pay you for both readings."

Ginny, to my surprise, shakes her head. "No, honey, that's okay. This one isn't finished, and I have a feeling you needed some advice more than I need the cash."

I haven't cried in a very long time. I learned relatively young that life is full of lemons, swift kicks in the pants, spilled milk, and all that, and crying about it does no good at all. So, it's saying a lot that right now, I can feel the hot pricks starting behind my eyes.

"Thank you. Really. You have no idea how kind of you that is."

When I make my way back out of the shop, I find Ash standing there. He didn't ghost me after all. He waited, which is kind of nice, except he doesn't look nice. His face looks stormy, and he's pale. His eyes are also darting all over the place like something sketchy is about to come at us.

"I'm calling an emergency meeting with my brother and cousins," he announces before stalking off down the street, leaving me to catch up.

6

ASH

Ellis follows me through the front door. She's been silent on the walk all the way home, her phone out in front of her, such that a couple of times, I had to double back to make sure she wasn't going to get hit by a car or a falling piano or something. Not that the latter is likely, but one never knows.

I let us back into the house through the front door, and it's a good thing because it's getting busy out there, though I don't know if NOLA is ever quiet. The weather tends to be quite lovely all year round, especially in comparison to other places, but as we're entering summer, things are seriously picking up. Including the temperature.

I realize, as a blast of AC hits me, I've soaked right through my t-shirt. To be fair, it might have happened during the card reading, before the sun ever started working its blistering magic on me.

I glance at Ellis, but she has her phone up in front of her face. She's using her left hand to hold it while scrolling with her right. My stomach plunges when I note the ring on her finger. It stares me down, as frightening as any mystical being suddenly come to life has a right to be.

"It says here," Ellis starts, scrolling her phone eagerly. "It says the Major Arcana...all those big, important cards you got in your reading, have companion cards. When a card's companion card comes up, you're supposed to pay attention to it. The Wheel of Fortune's companion card is the Magician, and they came up back to back, both right side up." She lowers her phone. "When that happens, you're supposed to take some real notice because it means the issue is a big one."

"I don't need cards to tell me that," I huff. "Obviously, the issue is dang-blasted *monumental*."

Ellis rams her phone into her pocket, and her brows knit furiously. "Why didn't you let her finish the reading?"

"Because the whole thing is just a setup. It's so fake that I couldn't handle it."

"Really?" Her face oozes skepticism, but not about the reading. "Why do you say it's fake?"

"Because we were there together, and she pulled The Lovers card. Come on. How absolutely rigged can it get?"

"The cards are figurative! They're open to interpretation. I looked it up while we were walking, and The Lovers isn't always about romantic crap. It's mainly about choices or internal struggle."

"I still say it's rigged."

Ellis walks over to the couch. I have the inside set up entirely with antique furniture. It's not very comfortable, but it was expensive. Also, it's tasteful, and it seems to fit the house just fine—well, the exterior, at any rate. The interior, on the other hand, is a strange mashup of modern and antique. I should have gone that direction with the furniture, but the new stuff just didn't speak to me.

"I want a change of clothes," she demands, crossing her arms. "If you're going to hold me prisoner, you need to provide for me. That means food, water, and clothing."

I shake my head and get out my phone. "That's just perfect. I'm going to call my brother and cousins. Lee is just about your size."

Her mouth drops, and her eyes flash in outrage. "Lee? You're going to dress me in some dude's clothing?"

"Lee. Short for *Leandra*."

"How should I know?" Ellis pulls out her phone again and shifts so her feet are propped up on a coffee table that is approximately a hundred years old and should never, ever have feet on it. I choke back a protest, not wanting to sound like a prude.

"I thought you knew everything about my family."

She ignores my sweetly biting tone and starts working on her phone again. Then, when I have my back angled just slightly away, my phone going to my ear, I see her flip me the bird. I whirl, but her hand disappears as quickly as it came. Did I just imagine it?

As the phone starts ringing, Ellis jumps up. "I'm going up to my room. I want to write some things down about the reading. You might not believe in it, but I think it might help. I need some time to process. So, uh, just let me know when to come back down. Unless you plan to have this meeting the way a speaker incites a mob to violence, and in this case, the mob consists of your brother and cousins, and the violence is cutting off my finger, then please, by all means, let me know so I can jump right out the window before you can catch me."

I can tell she's not going anywhere, and she's also seriously worried about her finger getting detached from her body. I hold the phone away from my face as it rings. "Don't worry. If I were to cut something, I'd go for your middle finger first. Yeah, I saw that."

"Oh really? You saw it? What about now?" She waves it in the air, high and wide, then back up high again. "Can you still see it?"

I turn my back and ignore her. I think we're both getting frustrated. Our tempers are reaching boiling point, and I need to calm down before things simmer over. Maybe being at odds with each other isn't helping. That seemed to be a common thread in the reading. Instead, we should be getting our shit together to problem-solve accordingly.

It's also why I'm calling my brother and cousins. I could seriously use their insight right now. A few calls later, my brother Kirian and my cousins Toren, Taylen, and Leandra, who is bringing clothes without even asking me why I might need women's clothing, are on their way for an emergency meeting called, "*WTF are we going to do about these curses?*" Curses being plural because my brother and cousins all have their objects already.

Granny gifted us all with our curses on the same day five Christmases ago. Quite a gift if you ask me. To do a thing like that, one would almost swear she hates us instead of loves us. Kirian got a necklace, Toren got a bracelet, Taylen got a brooch, which is probably the strangest, most vintage of all the cursed gifts, and Leandra got a set of earrings. I don't know what would happen if she lost one. God help me because I don't want to find out.

I guess because we're all so tight, my cousins and brother all basically arrive at the same time, even though they all drive over separately and don't live equidistance from me. They pour through the front door one after the other, each with a broody, worried expression. They seat themselves in the antique chairs in the living room, the boys on the sofa and Leandra on her favorite chaise even though it's uncomfortable as all heck.

The strangest part of it all is that my normally boisterous family is totally quiet. Maybe they sense the heavy black air in the room, or perhaps it's the curse at work. It doesn't want us to come up with something illogical, so it's impaired our ability to speak. I'm about to go and call Ellis to come into the room because she really should be here for this, but as she usually seems to be, she's two steps ahead of me. Which means about twenty behind really.

I hear delicate little steps approaching. She doesn't waste any time, and she certainly hasn't lost her ability to shock, I mean to speak. She leaps up on the coffee table, thank god with her bare feet, also thank god the thing is strong as an ox and built in an era where shit was meant to survive a full-on apocalypse. Ellis, her dark hair cascading down her back, sweeps her eyes around the room, taking in each one of my cousins and my younger brother. She looks as solemn as if I'd assembled everyone to start in on some kind of black magic ritual.

"Gentlemen and uh, lady," Ellis says in her best showman voice. "May I have your attention." She produces her hand, and the ring seems like it's grown in size. I know it's impossible, but all I see when I look at her finger is that bastard piece of jewelry. "The curse is real. Very. Real."

The room is literally so silent that if you dropped a pin —god who uses pins, but more like if someone dropped a very silent fart—it could probably still be heard before it smells.

"Well," Kirian says, looking askance at me. "That got dark really fast."

"I brought clothes," Leandra chimes in, holding out the

bag in front of her. She's put it in some grocery store cloth contraption, the kind of bags meant to save the planet.

My brother and all of my cousins are dressed in black. I guess, as a family, we like that color. Kirian is wearing a suit because he came right from work. He owns a security company. Toren and Taylen, who each hate their names and how similar they sound to each other, are twins in black t-shirts and faded jeans, and Leandra is wearing a black designer dress and pumps to match. She owns her own boutique. She has the same black sandy-hued hair and blue eyes as her brothers, or at least she used to. Her hair is now nearly platinum, and the dress outlines her body in a way that makes me, Kirian, and her brothers want to immediately get up and start kicking some ass because Leandra is the baby of the family. She basically has four older, protective brothers. Lucky girl.

Taylen ignores his sister and studies Ellis with a skeptical look. *Oh, no. Here we go.* "Who the heck are you?"

And then, as I suspected, all hell breaks loose, and the floodgates of questions pour forth.

"Ash's soulmate, apparently," Ellis states dryly. Her hands fly to her hips, and up on the coffee table, she looks like a strange statue of a bossy superhero.

The urge to paint her like that—her face fearless and undaunted, her eyes sparkling, the ring freaking glowing in the sun creeping through the big windows into the room, and her hair wildly tangled and finger-combed around her shoulders—is almost more than I can bear. My hand itches.

"No," I cut in, stepping forward. "No, she's kidding. She's my cleaner. Uh, a maid?" Does it sound bad to call a person a maid? I don't even know, and it makes her rich asshole accusations hit home. "It was an accident. This whole thing.

She's not my soulmate, and we are *not* in love. Or anything else. She's basically a stranger."

Ellis' lips curl back, and I know she's not going to make this easy for me. She looks directly at me. "A stranger who spent the night last night."

"In a separate room!"

Kirian groans. "So, you're one of those cliché douchebags who bangs their maid?"

"No!" Ellis looks at me smugly as I squirm on the spot. She's enjoying this far too much. I give her a sharp *this is not helping anything* look. "Do you think I would do that?" I give my brother a withering stare. "With her?"

"Thanks a lot," Ellis quips. "Totally standing right here."

"He's been keeping this on the down-low," Taylen says snarkily, elbowing his brother, who is choosing not to participate so far. Taylen looks back and forth between Ellis and me.

"What about Meryl?" Leandra goes there fearlessly.

"What happened?" Toren finally asks, the voice of reason.

"I just met her." Why do I feel the need to defend myself now? I haven't done anything wrong. "She's my maid. There was a mishap, and she put the ring on by mistake."

Taylen looks at me like he doesn't believe me, but lucky for me, the rest of the group is on my side. "How do you know it's real then?" he asks skeptically. "You can't know you're meant for each other. You're not soulmates, and you're not in love, so how has the curse come into play?"

"Because the ring won't come off," Ellis informs everyone. She slowly turns in a circle up there on the coffee table, holding out her hand. She tries to tug at the ring, but it doesn't budge.

Kirian gives us his expert medical advice without hesitation. "You must have swollen fingers."

Ellis looks up at the ceiling in exasperation. It must be extremely tough for her to deal with five rich a-holes instead of just one. "Thanks."

"We've tried everything," I say, stepping closer to the coffee table. I really want to get Ellis down from there for the sake of the table. Not because I want to set my hands on her curvy hips or get close enough to drink in the scent of any lingering perfume she might have put on yesterday or because I want to tangle my fingers in her hair, tip her face to mine, and take the proper time to explore her tantalizing mouth this time—*what the hell?*

"It's not a tight fit." Ellis' voice breaks through my line of WTF thoughts. "But it won't come off. We can't budge it." She swallows thickly. "We even had our cards read this morning-"

"No." I put up a hand, stopping her. "Don't get that involved. That was a bad decision."

"You did what?" Leandra leans forward, far more interested now. I swear, she thinks this curse thing is kind of a great idea even though she joined in our pact, with a little bit of coersion. Then again, Leandra is the least cynical out of all of us, though that's not saying much. "My most sensible cousin went for a card reading?" Leandra hoots, slapping her thigh. "How did you ever manage to drag him there?"

"Oh, he went willingly."

"Whoa, whoa, whoa." Toren puts up a hand. "Okay, so we all swore an oath not to believe in this curse. We said we wouldn't let it be real."

"Just from the outside looking in," Ellis starts cautiously, "I don't think you can prevent a curse or keep it from being real. You can be oblivious, but it's still probably going to come for you."

"Looks like the ring chose her," Kirian sighs. "You are soulmates whether you like it or not."

I swear this is some younger brother payback for all the times I was a mean older brother to him.

Taylen thinks that now is a good time to point out the obvious. "It's stuck on her now, so you're stuck with her."

"Hey!" Ellis stomps her foot, and the coffee table vibrates beneath her.

Leandra's eyes sweep back to me. "Does Meryl know?"

"Yes. She was here when it happened, but she's not pissed. You know Meryl."

Kirian leans back, tucking his hands behind his head. The bastard looks like he's ready to pop some popcorn since he's so thoroughly enjoying this drama. "Oh, so the ring didn't want to support a fake marriage?"

I glare at my brother. "No, that's still happening. And just because we're adults doesn't mean I can't give you a wedgie so hard, you'll cry."

Ellis' mouth drops open. "You gave your brother wedgies so hard that he cried? What is wrong with you?"

"Monster," Leandra echoes, shaking her head. She's biting down hard on her bottom lip to keep from grinning or laughing outright.

Kirian ignores my wedgie threats. He's bigger now, and he would fight back. He would try and rip my gotch off too, and I know it. "So, what are you going to do? Cut her finger off?"

Ellis stomps her foot, and the coffee table vibrates again. "Bah! Why does it always boil down to that?"

"Yeah, really. That's a little gory." Leandra pretends to gag.

"I think you should stay close." Toren grinds out, and we all stop fooling around and actually listen. Toren isn't the oldest cousin. He's two years younger than I am and just a few months older than Kirian, but he is generally quieter and has good things to say. He was always like that. I swear his IQ is off the charts, but he won't tell us. He does like to read, though—a lot. Always has. While the rest of us were twiddling our thumbs and mud-wrestling in the backyard with each other or gaming hard, Toren was working hard at getting smarter and wiser. "Close to each other, I mean. The curse is unpredictable if it is real. You shouldn't let her out of your sight until you can get the ring off because it might try to harm her. You should protect her."

Ellis throws up her hands and lets out a cry of joy. "At least there's one chivalrous one left."

I glare her down. "Care to expand on your theory about rich assholes?"

Instead of getting embarrassed as she should, Ellis just gives me a blank look. "What? I don't know what you're talking about."

"You called us rich assholes. Or me, and then you lumped my cousins and brother in."

"No." She shakes her head. "Never said anything like that. You must have misunderstood." Oh, she's good. She's smiling and all sweet and innocent up there. "It would be great if I could have some protection." She acts like she enjoys the idea of sticking close to me even though I know she can't stand me and only spent the night here last night because I threatened her with the police. "Although, from the card reading, at least what I gathered, the curse doesn't seem malevolent."

"You can't know that!"

Toren has been studying us the whole time, and he's

again the voice of reason. "I suppose the curse wouldn't choose our soulmates for us and then harm or kill them off."

"But you should probably take the night and think about things," Kirian adds. "I mean, what to do. We should each think about it and examine the objects Granny gave us. Maybe there are some clues there."

"Or maybe we should just talk to her and ask her who cursed them and where she got them," Leandra insists. "Wouldn't that make more sense?"

"No!" I very nearly panic. "You know how nosey Granny is. She would take so much glee in this. She can't find out. Not about Ellis, not about the ring getting stuck on the wrong person, and not about my, uh, well, how it really is with Meryl."

"She would be delighted. You're right." Leandra grins at me, enjoying my distress and discomfort way too much. I let my eyes rove over my brother and cousins.

"Just wait until it's your turn. You won't find it so funny then."

"Just because it happened to you does not mean it will happen to us as well. And, unlike you, we won't let anyone get close to our heirlooms." Kirian can't resist the urge to rub it in my face. "But don't worry, big bro." He knows I hate when he calls me that. "We'll help you out. We always do. Because we stick together. We're Cromwells. All of us." He casts a glance at Ellis. "Maybe even her?"

"Oh, no." She stomps her foot again, and I grind my teeth. "I'm drawing the line there. I'll never be a Cromwell." She spits our last name out like it's some foul brew she was forced to drink.

"You could always cut her finger off then," Taylen jokes, just to be an asshole.

"No!" The rest of us chime in unison.

Ellis' eyes sweep my face. They're wide, though I don't think she believes any of us would hurt her. She studies me for a minute, her eyes glistening and all misty. Then, without warning, she leaps off the coffee table and runs toward the stairs. I hear her thumping up every single one of them, and then the door to her room slams.

There is absolutely no way my brother and cousins are going to let me live this down, but for right now, only Kirian wants to be a smartass. "Looks like you handled that well." He stands, claps me on the shoulder, then pulls me into a brotherly bear hug. "Don't worry, big bro. We'll get it figured out. I mean, what's the worst that could happen? You find out she's your soulmate and fall in love with her anyway?"

"Not going to happen."

"We'll think on it." Leandra is next in line. She hands over the bag of clothes.

Toren and Taylen both slap me on the back. "Yup, we'll get it figured out," Taylen says.

"I'll read up on it," Toren promises. I have no idea how he's going to do that. It's not like the cursed items came with a guidebook.

"We could always go to Granny," Kirian says after they've moved off toward the door.

"No!" I cross my arms. "Not yet. Give me a chance to get it figured out. Granny is a last-ditch option for me."

Taylen can't resist one last jab. "I'm sure she'd be pleased to hear it at our next family dinner."

"Don't you dare tell her!"

"He'll threaten you with a wedgie next," Kirian mutters under his breath.

"I got enough of those growing up," Taylen groans. He gives me a warning look. "You try it, and I promise I will come here, get all your gotch, and hang them where everyone can see them. Oh, and I'll smear them with chocolate pudding, so it looks like there are weird stains going on."

Toren gives me a sympathetic look as they clear out. Leandra is the last one to go. She gives me the same look that, in a nutshell, says, I am so fucked, they all know it, and they're hoping like hell that the curse doesn't come for them next.

"I think you should go easy on her," she whispers. "You didn't even introduce her to us using her name. You just called her your maid. She was trying to be brave, but I can see she's scared. She's not a thing or a problem to be solved, Ash. She's a person with a life outside of here that got interrupted. She was sucked into this, and probably not by choice. Maybe you should give her a break and work together to try and solve the problem instead of going at war with each other."

"I would," I insist, feeling like a giant, hairy ball bag. "But she absolutely hates me for no reason at all. She really did call me a rich asshole."

She shakes her head. "So what? We've called each other a thousand things that are a thousand times worse over the years, and we all still love each other."

"She said it with malice. And we're not related. It's different."

"Whatever. Just get it figured out. And use a little more sensitivity. I know you have it in you."

Leandra leaves quietly after that. As a woman, she has a unique perspective the rest of us men don't have. I can see how she would sympathize with Ellis. It's not until after I shut the door that I realize Leandra's advice is pretty much like the reading we went to. Work together for a common goal and try and figure things out cooperatively. Wasn't that what it was saying? That seems to be what Ellis was trying to explain to me when she was talking about battling forces. Wasn't it?

I have no idea. I'm not built for this—all the emotional stuff, introspective crap, and soul searching. I stopped doing it a long time ago. I learned early to shut down and focus on the most productive emotions because life is real, and reality is a hard slap in the face sometimes, but there is nothing I can do about it other than survive. It's what led to the whole pact in the first place. Love isn't a thing, and I don't do that. I don't believe in it any more than I believe marriages can survive the test of time and humanity's general inclination to be assholes.

Right now, none of what I believe matters. There are feelings, and there are facts, and maybe Leandra was right. The fact is that Ellis is somewhere upstairs, and the ring is stuck on her finger, which sucks all around. And the truth is, maybe I could be less of a douchebag about it, so I guess I'll start there.

7

ELLIS

I know I left the room like a bit of a spaz, but I guess everything hit me all at once. I'm not one of those people who give in to tears, as I said, but again, they were suddenly threatening, and since I couldn't continue to be brave and advance into the great unknown with tears and snot dripping down my face, I retreated.

I don't know what it was that triggered the mountain of grief that suddenly leaped onto my shoulders. I tried to process it while standing at the window of the huge spare bedroom I slept in last night. A stranger's bed, a stranger's ring on my finger, a stranger's curse. And yet, honestly, it wasn't so bad. I actually had a great sleep—one of the best I've had in ages.

I watched Ash's cousins and brother leave out the front door. I guess maybe it was the way everyone kept looking at each other in the living room. There was some pretty clear emotion there. They might all be assholes or related to an asshole who is related to the assholes at the top, but the love they share was more than evident. All I felt, up on that coffee table, was the sharp pain of being the girl who didn't fit in again—the girl who was lost in her own life. I was right back to my thirteen-year-old self, learning how to start her life all over again after two huge losses.

I've been trying to keep it together for a long time. My grandpa died of a brain tumor, then a few years later, my mom was diagnosed with the same thing. My mom hung on for a year, but when she died, the pain of losing her as well was too much for my grandma, and she had a heart attack within two weeks of my mom's funeral. My dad, on the other hand, is estranged from his parents, so he never talks to them, and my aunts and uncles just kind of drifted away. They didn't know what to say or how to help us. It was a common trend. The newspaper was the only thing keeping my dad going. When he lost that, too, he kind of just climbed into this black hole.

A soft knock at the door surprises me. I figured Ash would leave me alone since it was pretty clear I wanted to be, and not having to deal with me is likely a relief for him. He follows his knock with my name, and for the life of me, I can't figure out what the shiver crawling up my spine at his soft tone is.

A shiver of stupidity, no doubt.

I walk over to the door, undo the lock, and pull it open. I can't hide in here forever. I remember, too late, that my face is full of dried tears, snot, and other less than appealing things. Ash blinks at me, stunned.

I swipe at my cheeks, surprised to find them still damp. "Wow," I mutter. "I must look like a mess."

He doesn't shut the door, but he does take a step forward. I retreat again, but he keeps coming. Finally, I stop, and so does he, and we just stare at each other. I know my gaze is probably burning with a whole lot of hot accusations and dislike, but his gaze is just blank. Like he doesn't know where to go from here.

Honestly, at the moment, with his jaw not clenched, his blue eyes so pale and tired-looking, and more than a shadow of dark stubble on his cheeks, he doesn't seem so much like an asshole. Not very much like an asshole at all...

Maybe that's just my brain. It's summoning up strange sensations because I'm emotionally exhausted. Or perhaps it's the ring manipulating my brain to send bad signals. Honestly, I have to blame the terrible connection on something, and when I do a double-take and drag my eyes over Ash's broad shoulders, his thick toned abs that can be seen through his soft t-shirt, and jeans that fit him sinfully well, my faulty brain seems like the best idea.

I have to remind myself that spontaneous ovulation is not a thing.

"Are you okay?" Ash's voice is deep, and it makes something in my insides quiver.

My eyes rise to his face. I'm too tired to blush at the fact that I was just perusing him like he's a billboard made to be stared at. "Why? Do I not look okay?"

That earns me a twitch of Ash's lips. Lips which I know for a fact, do not feel like kissing an asshole. Those lips on mine felt pretty good. He shakes his head and rakes a hand through his hair nervously.

"Right. Well, what if I'm just practicing reverse psychology, and this is my happy face?"

"It's not. I do understand basic human emotion, no matter what you might think. There is no mistaking the scathing looks you send my way. I know you don't like me. If I met my fiery demise falling into a flaming pit of doom right here, I think it would suit you just fine."

"Yeah, I'd probably be delighted." I can't keep a resting bitch face up. I have to crack just a little.

"You're sassy and spirited, and I have no idea how to deal with that, aside from everything else. After you left, my cousins suggested we work together to figure it out instead of working against each other."

"Gee, sounds like the cards."

His lips twitch again. "That's what I thought. Don't... don't tell me I told you so or anything. Just...I don't know why you hate me, but I was wondering if you could let it go for a little bit and focus instead on getting the ring taken care of so we can go our separate ways. But we should be nice to each other before that happens."

"I don't think you know how to be nice." It's too sassy, and I know it's shitting all over Ash's peace offering, but he doesn't take offense.

"Maybe I don't. But this..." He waves his hand over me from head to toe. "This isn't right. I don't know why you're crying. Well, actually, I can only imagine, given everything that's happened in less than twenty-four hours."

"It's not..." I stop. I don't talk about this. People get weird when I say things about my family, but I don't blame them. What is there really to say? I wouldn't be any better in their shoes. "Nothing." I shake my head. "It's just...you're right. This is hard." It's vastly better than admitting that the longing I felt watching five family members come together with great and obvious affection for each other nearly crippled me.

"You know what I think will fix it?"

"I can only imagine." I wipe my face again, smearing snot and tears all over the place. Good lord, I seriously need to wash my face and get cleaned up.

"Well, fresh clothes for a start. I had Leandra bring some over."

"We could have just driven over to my apartment together."

Ash's face falls. "Yeah, I didn't think of that."

"Because you're an asshole," I say without heat. In the joking kind of way that will make him think I don't think of him that way anymore. Suddenly and without warning. But deep down, I still do. Because it's a fact, and facts are always true. Right? I do still think of him that way. I swear I do.

His lips twitch for a third time. Getting a genuine smile out of him is harder than I thought. Not that I want to do that. Because I don't care if he smiles or not, and certainly, if he did, the brightness of it would not pierce through the dark of night, storm clouds, grief, or my lady bits. Nope. Just nope.

"Perhaps. Maybe. I uh...can probably be insensitive sometimes."

"Just sometimes?"

"Okay, I didn't think of going to your place to get a change of clothes. I'm sorry. But I did ask my cousin to bring some over. She owns a high-end boutique, selling clothing and shoes and stuff. The bag's downstairs, so you can check it out. I did look through it, and I think you'll like what she brought over. You can keep it."

My lips part, but no sound comes out. Suddenly, my mouth is so dry that I can barely swallow, but inside, I feel wet and mushy.

"I took the price tags off so it can't be returned, but also so you won't feel guilty. Or accuse us of being rich and throwing money around. It was a gift. You can call me an asshole if you like, but my brother, although it kills me to say it because he was annoying as hell growing up, and my cousins, who were also just as annoying as hell, are good people. They always were, and they've become good adults. We might have our issues, and yes, we have money, but it doesn't make us devoid of feelings. If you want to think of me as the worst of all of them, I can handle that. But give them a break. Please."

Suddenly, I feel like the asshole. My recorder is hidden under the bed, and I feel like it's burning a hole through the floor, announcing my guilt. No matter how much I work with Ash on getting the ring off, I'm still going to betray him after, even if I find out that he's maybe not as bad as I thought. I have to. I have to because vengeance is the only thing that can...can what? Save my dad? Make him less depressed? Bring back my mom and the past decade of my life that I've spent missing her? Justify anything at all?

Holy ballsacks, what the heck is happening to me?

I nervously bring my right hand up to my left and try and twist the ring because it seems like something good to work at, but it doesn't budge. It just makes the skin of my finger burn when I try and grasp it, though not an irregular burn. Just an *I'm not going anywhere, so quit trying to pull me off or play with me* kind of a burn. It slightly mirrors what's going on in my twisted up, churning insides.

"What did you say would fix this?" I ask while staring down at the floor. I don't tell Ash that I'm going to have to leave sometime tonight or tomorrow to check on my dad.

Because he's alone, and I'm worried about him. I go to his house every other day to do some meal prep and cleaning and also try and get him to say something. Anything.

My boss knows where I am, so I don't have to worry about that. My apartment is pretty barren and soulless because I have no one depending on me—no one who would be sad if I suddenly had to leave to go somewhere. I've made it that way, I realize. No cat, no dog, no bird or fish, and no plants. I always wanted to be a journalist, and I wanted to work with my dad—working side by side with him, writing stories that made a difference, and making him proud. Instead, I write for a sleazy, online publication that just wants to rock the clickbait and would pass up anything with any sort of meaning because *meaningful* isn't what they're in the business of.

"Food," Ash announces proudly.

My head jerks up. "Food?" I'm not even hungry. I can't be hungry when I'm drowning in emotions because it makes me completely nauseated.

"But I have to admit all I have in the fridge is healthy stuff you wouldn't like. I know because I can barely stomach it. If you don't want some juiced-up grasses and vegetables, then I suggest we order something before the hanger gets real."

"Order something?" I hate that I sound so dumb, but all I want to do is wash my face.

"I can get something, anything. Just not something fried. It has to be semi-healthy."

"Hard pass."

Ash makes a sound in his throat, and I finally look up at him. He's trying. He really is. Something in me softens even though I want it to stay hard as iron, resolute as granite, and stubborn as sludge. All that good stuff. Or should I say, bad stuff, such as dislike. That's what I need to cling to. Not this creeping warmth that is slowly invading all the crevices, cracks, and also big deep holes that I know are inside me. And not just physically either but mentally and emotionally, too. All the real crackly cracks, holy holes, and creaky crevices.

"Art then!" Ash blurts, looking me right in the eye. I think he realizes that a challenge is something I will always rise to. "You said you could create something better, so I'll get the canvas set up and the paints ready. Then, I'll go order food, and you can get started."

"Just because art is a crutch that makes you..." The words die, strangled in my throat. I feel all soft and melty inside, but old evils die hard. "Sorry. Just...that's not...forget it. We're not doing that anymore, being mean. But it's going to take some practice."

"It's fine." Ash shrugs. "I've used it in the past to deal with all sorts of stuff. I think a lot of people do that. Isn't that where everyone says good art comes from? Places of pain?"

"Uh, I wouldn't know. I think people can make good art when they're in good moods."

"Maybe. Probably."

"But you are right. Even in a good mood, they're probably drawing on past experiences and sources of pain. Things that made them think about something deeply, something that inspires them, something they came through. So I guess maybe both?"

"This is getting deep."

"Yeah," I mutter as I scrub my face. "Alright. Go set up the studio or whatever and make sure I can't do any harm by flinging paint around on the rest of your canvases." An evil grin tugs at my lips. "Although, I'm sure it would be an improvement. I'm going to wash up."

"That's a good idea, but keep those clothes on. You'll get messy, I warn you. You'll need a second wash up."

I tilt my head down, suddenly so embarrassed that Ash is seeing me like this, I can hardly stand it. I mean, I was embarrassed before, but geez. I must look truly nasty. I never let anyone see me like this. In fact, I never even let myself see myself like this, so I draw on my inner snarky and find comfort in the sassy me that I can usually effortlessly channel.

"Uh, how long will it take for the food to get here?"

"Maybe half an hour?" Ash shrugs. One big shoulder goes up, and his t-shirt flexes and tightens over his abs. A hint of bronzed skin shows between the hemline and the beginning of his jeans, and suddenly, it's even harder to swallow. "Why?"

"I'll be finished by then."

"The painting? Your painting?"

"Yeah." I look up at him with my dried tears, nasty snot, and all. I'm finding my sass and reclaiming it, and it feels good. I can be strong without being mean, can't I? Yes! Yes, I can. And I'm going to. "What? Afraid I'll outdo you?"

"I have no doubt the masterpiece will be museum-worthy in under thirty minutes." The biting sarcasm is very obvious, and I rise to it with glee.

"No doubt it will be vastly superior to anything you've ever created."

Ash walks to the door. He grips the doorframe and turns, and I swear I see his eyes dancing with humor. Maybe he just really likes art. Or it could be that I'm not the only one who likes a challenge. "I wouldn't be so cruel as to set you up for failure, but if you want to do it yourself, I'm not going to stop you." He drops that and leaves, and somehow, he does it all without sounding like his old, combative, not-so-nice self.

For a minute, he has this sort of soft, serene expression on his face, and it nearly makes me panic because it almost looks like he wants to come back into this room and do something crazy, like hug me. I can imagine his strong arms wrapping around me, holding me close, and I can imagine fisting my hands in his shirt and dragging him to me. My body becomes instantly shivery, my nipples and ovaries pulsing—if they can pulse because they certainly feel like they can—my palms damp, and my breathing erratic.

Luckily, Ash turns and leaves before anything crazy can happen. I mean, crazier than us not being adversaries. Are we really on the same team now? It's so freaking hard to imagine, but then I glance down at the ring, and I get it. This is just for the ring. It's all for the ring. It doesn't have anything to do with us personally. I think. Tomorrow, I can still go back to wanting to explore him like a new asshole. I mean, tear into him like the asshole he is. Holy guacamole, this curse is warping my mind.

What's wrong with me that I feel a bubble of excitement? I shouldn't be looking forward to any bit of this other than handing in a story that wrecks Asherly Cromwell's life. I know I've said it once, but I'll say it again. The curse is real. Very, very real. And I'm hardcore blaming it for what happens from here on out.

8

ASH

By the time the food gets here—a stir-fry because it's both delicious and healthy—it's been forty minutes, so I head upstairs to check on my new artist's masterpiece.

Maybe part of me is worried she'll outdo me. Or I'm just scared to go up and talk to Ellis because I'm starting to wonder if maybe a new madness is taking hold of me, erasing doubts and sanity and good judgment. Halfway up the stairs and down the hall to the large room I use as my studio, I'm already thinking of Ellis in there, working on a canvas and bringing it to life. The thought of her flinging paint all over the place is far more erotic than it should be.

It kind of steals my breath and makes Mr. Happy in my pants quite a bit happier than he was a few seconds ago. *Why on earth did I just call my dick Mr. Happy?* I have never *ever* thought of it that way before. But with Ellis around, it kind of seems to have taken a life of its own.

I push open the door and find Ellis hard at work, but what she's doing in there could hardly be labeled a masterpiece, and I'm quite liberal with my taste in art. She whirls away from the large canvas I set up for her. Anything can be painted over, so it didn't bother me to let her use one. Her eyes get all big and doe-like when she spots me. Even though she scrubbed her face after her crying session, which still stabs me in the gut, paint splatters have replaced the tears. She has paint in her hair, paint entirely coating her clothing, and paint on the floor, the walls, the easel. The canvas too, but that's the expected bit.

Ellis bites down hard on her bottom lip, and I have the sudden impulse to abandon everything that's rational, tug her to me, and get very dirty. I mean paint. Paint kind of dirty. I want to transfer all that color between us. I know it's utter madness, but so is the confusion and discombobulation I feel by just looking at her. God, she's beautiful.

That's it. I've lost my senses entirely.

It's the curse. Day two is apparently much more potent than day one.

"I...uh...it's harder than I thought," Ellis stammers.

She gnaws at her bottom lip, and I'd very much like to replace her teeth with my tongue and do that for her. The temptation is so great that I nearly cross the room. I have to latch onto the doorframe and curl my fingers hard into the wood to keep myself from crossing the room. And lines. And boundaries.

"Would this be the appropriate time to say I told you so?"

"It would be the appropriate time to tell me where I can get cleaned up and where the change of clothing is." She eyes the canvas, which is coated first in black paint and is dripping every shade of color I have and then has some bigger, thicker blobs randomly interspersing the surface.

"Are you going to paint over that?" She squints at me, and a muscle in her forehead throbs. "I can smooth it out, so it isn't all lumpy. I'd hate for you to waste a good canvas."

"Yeah." But I already know there is no way in the hottest of hells I'm going to cover it up. I'll put it somewhere so I can look at it every single day and remember this exact moment. The exact shade of golden brown of Ellis' eyes—somewhere between sea and setting sun—the tilt of her pink lips, the flush on her alabaster skin, and the paint smears on her t-shirt just over the swell of her breasts beneath.

Too far. Wayyyyy too far. Stop at the eyes, man. The lips are pushing it. And don't go below the neck.

"Uh..." I feel very out of sorts. But I bet it's the hunger. It has to be. Hunger can be blamed for so much. Low blood sugar is a real bitch, so I feel pretty confident about using it as a legit excuse. "Right. The bathroom. Uh, it's down the hall. I already put the bag of clothes Leandra brought in there. The food is here too, but I'll keep it boxed up until you get to the kitchen, so it stays warm."

A vein throbs in Ellis' forehead, though I'm not sure why because I'm being nice. I guess maybe it makes her surly. Or it could just be the hunger getting to her too. We haven't eaten all day, and it's getting late. Plus, the curse is a lot to deal with. It's enough for anyone to work up a massive appetite.

I let Ellis brush past me. She heads straight to the bathroom, darts in, and shuts the door. I wait with every single muscle tensed up until the shower starts. Wishing I was in there is just wrong, and wishing I was kissing away water droplets and washing paint out of her hair is even worse. Instead of thinking taboo thoughts like a creep, I force myself to get to work cleaning up the studio. It's a real mess, and it'll take hours to straighten up, but I put away what I can and bring down the few brushes Ellis used before getting them cleaned in the mudroom off the kitchen. I have a big industrial sink in there where I usually do all my cleanup. The paint is acrylic, so it washes out of everything quite easily. I'm not sure about Ellis' t-shirt and jeans, though, so I might have to reimburse her for those.

I'm down by the kitchen, cleaning up brushes and inhaling the heavenly scent of freshly cooked vegetables and stir-fry spices wafting into the mudroom when I hear a shriek come from upstairs. I drop the brushes and hoof it up there so fast that I nearly trip twice on the stairs. I stop short of the bathroom door when I see Ellis appear.

"What is it?" I gape at her, my heart pounding.

"This!" She smooths her hand over a tightly fitted black dress. It's a little black dress, to be more specific, and it fits her jaw-droppingly well. My mouth dries up, and other things stand at attention, saluting Leandra's choice.

The dress looks totally different on Ellis than her jeans and t-shirt did. It outlines her full breasts, pushing them up without the neckline being too low, and it hugs Ellis' tiny waist and curvy hips. Also, the dress is quite short on her but definitely enough to cover her bottom, which is too bad. I mean, which is tasteful. Ellis is likely somewhere around five-seven, but in that dress, her legs seem to go on forever. She has beautiful legs. Insanely gorgeous legs. Legs a man could get lost in. Between. Legs that would be the perfect complement when wrapped around my hips... Now I think I need to dick-punch and facepalm myself because I am going off on tangents I have no right to be thinking about.

Although...that dress. That dress makes me want to think about and explore every single tangent, ever.

Ellis' hair is still dripping wet, and the droplets slide over her arms and shoulders, soaking the top of the dress. One lands right below her neck and trickles down into the land of forbidden fruits. *Forbidden fruits? I'm losing my mind.*

Or my grip on reality and my sanity. Because I want to haul her up against me and kiss her breathless. I want to rip that dress off and see if she got every little bit of paint scrubbed away. I think there was something I needed to tell her, unrelated to any of that, but now my mind is totally blank.

Ellis tugs at the hem of the dress uncomfortably. "This is ridiculous. After we eat, we have to go to my apartment and get some clothes. I can't wear this."

"Yes, your place. Um, go. Yes, we will. Food. Yes, downstairs."

Ellis looks at me like I might have just sprouted a dick from my forehead. Because she's looking at my face, not at my waist, and she still seems equally disgusted and unsure. She's probably brain-scanning me and reading all my taboo thoughts about ripping off her clothes and finding out what exact shade of color her nipples are. I'm an artist, so I know my colors. I imagine they'd be a dark raspberry swimming in a sea of alabaster cream.

It's official. I have legitly divorced myself from my own sanity.

"Food. Yes. Okay." Ellis nods. She gives me another strange look then walks away, leaving me there practically panting and drooling in a puddle. I can smell the scents of my shampoo and body wash. Spicy. Invigorating.

Those scents are now on Ellis' skin and in her hair. Lord. God. *Get a grip, corndog. I mean horndog.* Right. Food, downstairs, eating. Then clothes for Ellis. Then back to trying to figure out the cursed ring.

I somehow make it down the stairs without toppling over from being so dick-heavy in the front—I swear a raging erection can throw you off balance quite easily. I don't fall on my face, and I don't trip over my feet on the way to the kitchen. I have zero shit under control when it comes to my dick, but I manage to edge myself around the island while Ellis is putting food onto two plates. It still smells divine, but not as good as I now know she smells.

I just have to give up on this because my thoughts are going to think, and my body is going to react, and my dick is going to...well, I can only imagine. Apparently, I can't stop it, so I go into immediate action, trying to do damage control, which means continuously standing behind the island, so it hides me from the waist down, eating like that, and trying not to look at Ellis. Or inhale her, which is hard. Her delicious scent is barely masked by the smell of peppers and onions. And that's saying a lot because peppers and onions are potent beasts.

"Are you alright?" Ellis asks as a noodle dangles from her fork. She slurps it into her mouth like a pro, and I'm impressed. "You look funny. I swear, if you poisoned this, I'm going to kill you."

"If I poisoned myself, you'll kill me?"

"Uh, I guess I didn't think that through."

"No." Ellis spears some broccoli and brings it to her mouth. Has anyone ever looked so deliciously tantalizing while eating broccoli? Not that I can remember. "But I'm glad you agreed to finally let me leave the house."

I crunch down hard on a water chestnut. "I'm driving."

"I should have known there was a catch." She doesn't look mad. Instead, she just looks resigned.

I guess the conversation about being on the same team must have sunk in. Maybe we both want to figure out the curse that badly. Ellis suddenly sighs and sets her fork down, and I'm instantly alert because a new sadness has crept into her eyes and is filling them, making them all golden and teary, and I don't like it. I'm not into being a superhero, where I fix all the bad in the world, but for just this one moment, I wish I could be. I wish I could fix all the stuff that makes Ellis sad. And I don't even know her. I don't know what any of it could be, but I want to.

I set my fork aside too. I didn't realize it, but I'm nearly finished. I guess when a person's extra hungry, hoovering up food is a real thing. Somehow, an entire plate of stir-fry just disappeared. The hairs on the back of my neck stand on end. Curse? Is that you? My stomach rumbles, and no, I guess it was just me.

"Hey...what is it?"

Ellis' eyes start twitching. Both of them. I have never seen anyone capable of doing that, and my god, it must be uncomfortable. "What's what?"

"You look sad right now. And you're not eating."

"You noticed? Hmm." She twists the ring on her finger and studies it thoughtfully. Now, something is twitching in her temple—a vein. And it's throbbing in time with her eyes.

"Ouch. That looks uncomfortable."

"What does?"

"The...your eyes...your forehead..." She looks at me, baffled. "Uh, never mind. But you do look sad. I...will you tell me what's wrong?"

Her lips thin, and she picks up her fork and plays with her food. Thank goodness, because if she's moving stuff around on her plate, it means she's not sticking the fork into my eye. "Nothing," she finally whispers in a way that means everything, but she clearly doesn't want to talk about it, and she's not just being mopey for my sake. This is some real dark shit she's dealing with.

"There's something wrong."

"Okay." Her head jerks up, and the fork stops. I judge the

distance between her plate and my eye and back up a step. "Other than the curse? Other than the fact that I'm basically a prisoner? Other than...ugh, never mind. There isn't any point in going over this. I just...there are some things I want to keep private. After we go to my apartment, I need to check on my dad. He'll be wondering what happened to me. I can't just call or text, and I'm not going to explain why that is. It's something I want to do alone."

"I'm not letting you go alone." Right. So, apparently, I've now adopted the white knight in shining armor, prince coming to save the damsel-in-distress persona. "The curse! I mean, it's unpredictable, right? Until we figure it out, I think we shouldn't split up. I'll drive you. I can wait in the car."

Ellis wears skepticism well. But then again, I think she wears all looks well. And t-shirts and jeans. And form-fitting little black dresses. "Isn't that still splitting up?"

"At least I'll be close by if shit goes down."

She moves her hands to her hips. "What kind of shit do you anticipate happening?"

"I think it's better not to brainstorm. It might give the ring strange ideas."

"Oh really?" she snorts sarcastically.

"Finish your stir-fry, and let's hit the road."

"I changed my mind. You're not just a rich asshole. You're a bossy, commanding, self-centered, witty but not in a good way, blustering, controlling rich asshole."

"Mmmhmm. Okay. I really do just want to keep you safe."

"Yeah, right."

I nod and finish off the rest of my food like I'm a vacuum. "So," I say as I wipe my face with a napkin. If someone tells you it's possible to eat stir-fry in a dignified manner, and it contains noodles, they are straight-up lying.

"I noticed your new description of me didn't contain the fact that I'm a bad artist. You must have changed your tune after you gave it a try."

"Whatever," Ellis mumbles, twirling her noodles with her fork. "I'm not going to give you the satisfaction, so don't even bother."

"The satisfaction of what?"

"Of validating your art. I still think it looks like garbage."

"But skilled garbage, you have to admit."

I think I see her lips twitch, and an insane bolt of even more insane happiness goes straight to my gut like someone just threw a lightning rod at me. Who is the god of storms again? Zeus? Bastard.

"I'm not admitting anything."

"Do I detect a hint of grudging respect?"

"You detect a hint of this." She holds out her left fist and cranks with her right, and slowly, her middle finger comes up. All I can see is the ring on her finger. My ring.

Ellis picks up her fork and tackles the rest of her food. *Slurppppp.* A noodle smacks her straight in the forehead since she sucks so hard. I barely hold in a laugh. She picks it off, puts it to the side, and keeps going without batting an eye.

Wow. What a freaking woman! I've never met anyone who could get a noodle wet willy and not bat an eye. I stand there watching Ellis in that tight black dress, a dress I think Leandra might have purposely chosen because she wanted to play a joke on me or get me back for all those times I messed up her dates by scaring off potential—asshole—boyfriends.

Ellis doesn't seem to mind at all that I'm watching her, and her confidence is crazy inspiring. She might be infuriating, but she's also just so...so *unique.*

"Alright then, if you're driving, let's go. But you have to promise to wait in the car. If you don't, I swear I will chop *your* finger off and make you eat it."

"Ouch. Well, on the list of things that could be cut off, I suppose that's one of the more merciful body parts."

I have my keys hanging by the front door even though the garage is closer to the back way out of the kitchen. I guess I've always walked around the house to get there, and I have no idea why. The whole thing is shaped funny, but I guess it's what I get when I buy an ancient historic house in a historic part of the city. Garages came later, and they have to go where there's room to stick them, which is preferably out of sight because tourists don't like to look at things like that. So yes, my garage is located around the back, just off the fenced backyard. It's only a two-car garage, but again, sacrifices must be made if I want to live here. And I do. All my life, I wanted a house in the French Quarter. I didn't need it as validation since I was rich my whole life. I just...I don't know. Liked it and wanted it. I love NOLA, and to me, this is the heart of the city. Even if it's not the typical idea of someone's dream house and location when thinking about a rather unlimited budget, it is mine.

Ellis follows. Thank goodness, because if I had to watch her walk in that tight-fitting dress, I don't think I'd make it. As it is, I have to wonder if driving with a hard-on might be an actual hazard. Because of loss of blood flow to the brain and all that. At the very least, it's distracting, embarrassing, and annoying. *Thank you very much, rock hard freaking erection that won't deflate and will not listen to logic and reason.*

Ha. Well, whaddya know. I guess I found something else to focus on besides the curse.

9

ELLIS

I know I shouldn't let Ash drive me over to my dad's. I should go on my own. Sometimes I'm there for hours, though, and sometimes for longer if things aren't going well. I don't want to be distracted by Ash calling me constantly. I also don't want him sitting at the curb for hours, but maybe because he's out there, karma will for once not be a bitch and let Dad be having a good day.

I don't say a thing as Ash drives us over to my dad's. It's not far from my apartment. I was fast up there. I threw a few shirts and pairs of pants into a duffel bag, grabbed my toothbrush and other toiletries, packed my laptop, and I was out of there. I don't have anything to look after, so I can be fast. I'm glad Ash didn't come up to see the sad state of my apartment. It's not very homey, and I can't even say I just moved in. I've had the place for a few years, and it's alright, I guess, though not in the best area of New Orleans. I don't consider it home. I don't consider my dad's house home either. In fact, I don't consider anywhere to be home, and maybe that's a problem, but I don't let myself think about it. I tended to bury myself in school and then work. I also have enough friends that I can be busy if I want to be. I'm hardly ever home. Who needs art on the walls, a nice friendly cat, or comforting things like plants? I have books, and they've always been my escape, so that's good enough for me.

"Are you sure you don't want me to come in?" Ash eyes me skeptically when we pull up to the curb. One of his dark brows nearly goes up to his hairline when I shake my head. "It's not a good neighborhood."

"Yeah. Got that. I grew up here. I'm good."

"Are you sure, sure?"

"Hey," I snap. I turn toward Ash, counting to ten in my head because everyone says that crap works. "Just because we're on the same team for a little while or something doesn't mean I won't ask this curse for some powers, laser beams, or like some kind of black smoke from my hands. Smoke balls? Anyway, I'll try and develop that just so I can obliterate you if you leave this car."

"Whoa." Ash holds up a hand. "Okay. Gotcha. No leaving the car."

I slide out, and before I shut the door, I lean in and say, "You might want to lock the doors. It's not a good neighborhood."

This time, Ash rolls his eyes. Maybe I'm rubbing off on him. Better than him rubbing off on me. Or up on me. My ovaries nearly rocket through my brain when I think about Ash doing any such thing, even when I imagine him on all fours, rubbing my ankles like the cat I don't have. Is it wrong that even that's hot?

I lose all sense of humor and all the hot and bothered shivery stuff the second I walk through the front door. I have a key. It's always on my keyring, so I let myself in. As usual, all the blinds and curtains are shut, and most of the lights are off. I know Dad's at home since he doesn't go anywhere if he can help it. I also see the evidence of some major at-home living. The back door opens into the kitchen. At least the dirty dishes overflowing the sink tell me that dad's eaten something these past few days. I quickly check the fridge and find it nearly full, so I'm not sure what Dad eats. I go through it quickly, pulling out anything that's rotten or on the verge of getting there. A bag of salad that has morphed into green slime goes into the trash. An old loaf of bread I find at the back is now more fuzz than actual bread, so it hits the trash too. I open a few jars of jam since I haven't remembered to check those for a while, and when I find them farming their own farms on top of what looks to be red sludge below, they hit the trash as well.

With the fridge properly purged, I walk into the living room, where I know I'll find my dad melted into his armchair. I swear the thing is shaped around him now. There's a big dad-sized dent in it whenever he gets up. He's slumped over, the room dark, the light from the TV doing paranormal kinds of things to the room.

"Dad?" He never greets me even though he knows I'm here, and he never gets up to check and see what I'm doing to his fridge. It's in the back of my mind that I still need to tackle the dishes. "Dad?" I reach for the side table, grab the remote, and switch off the TV. The room is plunged into total darkness, so I have to go to the wall and flick the switch before I can even find my dad to talk to him.

The light gets his attention in that retina-burning kind of way people get after sitting in the dark for too long. He blinks at me, his red-rimmed, bloodshot eyes watering a little.

"Oh. Ellis," he says, staring at me blankly as if he can't quite figure out what I'm doing there. Or maybe it's just because the details of my face haven't registered in his brain yet since his eyes are still focusing, and he's asking if it's me and not someone intent on burgling the home.

"Yeah, Dad, it's me." The room is fairly clean, but I was just here a couple of days ago to tidy it. The house is practically a time capsule from the seventies. Nothing has been changed. Certainly not the hairy brown carpets or the yellow and orange wallpaper. The décor is more modern because my mom had a hand in it, and my dad hasn't changed anything. The big velvet painting with the cactus still hangs over the TV and the TV stand, while the couches are the same brown suede. My dad's chair came with the set, so it's brown suede too. The coffee table has a massive stack of books, magazines, food wrappers, and other garbage on it.

Dad's clothes are rumpled and stained. He lives in gray sweats and white t-shirts, except they're not so gray and white anymore, and I know for a fact that he didn't do a change-up on me since I've been here last and put on another set of old, stained clothes to try and trick me into thinking he'd changed. Dad doesn't care about tricking me. He doesn't care how much of this I see. I think he gave up on trying to hide that aspect of his life a long time ago.

"Have you eaten tonight?" I ask patiently, moderating my voice, so it's not scolding.

"Yup." Dad stares longingly at the dark TV screen.

I sigh. "Turn it back on. I'll go and tackle the dishes."

He doesn't need me to tell him twice since he was in the middle of his favorite true crime show. Dad loves that stuff. He always wanted to be an investigative journalist. I guess he was for a while before he started his own publication. I don't want to go down that road again because it just leads to potholes and eventually a big drop off into a pit of absolute shit. I randomly look down at my left hand and swirl the ring on my finger.

Wait? Swirl? The thing actually *swirled*? I think a miracle is about to occur, but like all miracles, it's just another big middle finger flying in my face while the universe has a good laugh at me. The ring doesn't budge. I try to swirl it again, but nope. Apparently, it's done all the movement it plans on doing. I look at Dad, already absorbed back into his show. At least it's in the courtroom phase and not the bodies phase. Ew. I never liked that kind of stuff. I find it graphic and disturbing. Coming here is pretty much my threshold for how much I can put up with, and hearing about other people's lives gone so horribly wrong in so many violent ways is too much. Our lives don't need that extra bit of seasoning. We're already spicy enough, and by spicy, I mean fucked over by grief.

I head to the kitchen and start on the pile of dishes. To say they're really gross is an understatement, especially since my dad doesn't appreciate the fine art of soaking anything after he uses it. I'm still scrubbing away, somehow thoroughly soaked, when the door creaks open. I instantly grab a frying pan, but it's the last person on earth who should ever step foot in this place, not a robber.

"What are you doing in here?" I hiss. My fingers are still curled menacingly around the frying pan's handle.

Ash looks around at the kitchen. Then his eyes travel to me. "A sketchy car drove past me full of thugs. You were taking a while, so I wanted to come in and make sure everything was okay.'

"What? Did you think I was doing something nefarious in here? Or getting it done to me? This is a decent neighborhood, for your information. I mean, just because people have to do things you've never heard of before, like budgeting, coupon-cutting, and all that, doesn't mean they aren't good people."

Ash skips right over my offended and angry look and just gives me an exasperated one. "Stop," he says in the kind of tone that tells me he's about done hearing about how he's a rich douchebag. He looks around the kitchen but thankfully can't see into the living room because of the way the wall is angled. "You said you were checking in on your dad. Is he okay?"

I start scrubbing hard at a pot that looks like a murder happened in it, but then, when does dry red sauce not look like that? Obviously, my dad's true crime shows are rubbing off on me. "Yup, he's fine."

"The house is dark."

"Yup, it's dark."

"Uh...Ellis? Are you going to tell me what's going on in here?"

I ignore him and keep scrubbing.

"Do I have to call you Elisa to get a response?"

"You know what?" I pull my hands out of the sink, and they're dripping ominous red suds. I probably look a little crazed with my shirt soaking wet and hair damp because of the steam from the sink and how many times I've pushed it out of my face with my soapy hands. "Just go back and wait in the car. Please. I'm almost done. I need ten more minutes, and whatever inconvenience I've been to your day will be over."

"That's not what I was thinking, and you know it."

The strangest thing is it almost looks like the ring on my finger is glowing for a second, but it's probably just the kitchen light I cracked on when I came in and the suds and nasty red sauce bits floating in the sink. And the fact that I also don't smell old dishes but something piney, woodsy, and manly that's definitely wafting off of Ash, and I'm getting all hot and piney in my woodsy—okay, that's just a very wrong play on words—doesn't mean it's the curse acting up. It just means my olfactory bits are going haywire.

I go for the magic P since please is about all that's left to me at the moment. "Please," I rasp. "Just give me ten minutes."

"I can wait here..." He motions to the table in the corner that's overflowing with unopened mail, old bills—things I still have to sort through—and other random dirty dishes I haven't swiped yet.

I shake my head. "Outside. Please." He must hear the strain in my voice and realize how close I am to the old-fashioned breaking point. Part of me, the evil and extremely sinister part I try not to listen to very often, wants to tell Ash to go around the corner and introduce himself to my dad. I want to tell Ash to take a good, hard look at my dad because it was his life his family ruined. I wanted him to look at the aftermath, to see what a shell of a person looks like. To see what stripping away the last precious thing to a man does to him.

Honestly, though, it's been a long day as it is, and the rage just isn't in me. It's there, but it's not at my disposal. I'm like a shaken bottle of champagne where the cork stays in, and the bubbles of rage don't come flying forth even though they're super freaking close.

"Okay. But in ten minutes, I'm coming back in."

I nod. "Right. Ten minutes."

Ash lets himself out, and I go back to madly scrubbing dishes. I'm not going to process this right now. I can do that later in a rather comfortable bed in a strange guest room while I'm not sleeping because who can sleep when they've been cursed and just about everything else in their life has gone to straight shit? It's rhetorical. The answer is no one.

I finish up the dishes, even the dirty ones from the table, and go check in on my dad one last time. "I'm leaving," I announce while the TV flickers oddly in the room. I don't look at it. I sense there are bodies on there, and I'm just so done. Dad doesn't even turn his head. "Dad?"

"Okay," he says passively. He doesn't even blink as the lights flash across his face.

"Dad?"

"Hmm."

I glance down at the ring. I really, really want to tell him what happened. I need him to listen, to tell me that somehow, everything will be okay. "I'll be back in a couple of days to check on you, okay?"

"Yup. Thanks."

"Can you...do you think maybe we could do something together when I come over? Have dinner? Here?"

"Yes."

I know he means no. Or maybe he does mean yes, but I know it won't happen. I can't remember the last time I did something normal with my dad. It was when he still had his paper, and everything wasn't good, but it was still better than it is now. That was the last time.

I place a kiss on my dad's forehead and let myself out. I feel as heavy as I do after every single time I leave here. Everyone talks about the sins of the father, but the things that happened to my dad weren't sins as it's not the sins being visited on me. Rather, it's the burdens because I feel the burden of my dad's grief, his loss, and what he sees as his failure. If the house wasn't paid off, I know my dad would lose it. As it is, he doesn't have much of his savings left to keep covering the bills, and he has no health insurance. We're just one step away from a big fucking disaster, and I feel the burden of that too.

As I walk down the driveway and back to the car, I somehow manage to have my head lifted like I have a bit of my pride left. I slip into the passenger seat and wear my seatbelt as Ash looks at me, a thousand questions brimming in his eyes. The car smells like him—rich and manly. If muscles had a smell, then the car would smell like male muscles. As it is, even with all the pine swirling deliciously around me like the blue smoke of a fragrant fire deep in the woods with a thousand tall trees overlooking it, I ignore Ash. I turn my face to the window and say nothing the rest of the way home.

Not home. I meant back to Ash's house. To the French Quarter.

10

ASH

Ellis might have been silent in the car, but when we enter the house via the living room and not the kitchen—thank god because it lacks sharp and heavy objects—she turns and lets me have it.

"Why couldn't you just wait in the car?"

I'm not getting into a blazing fight with her even though I can see by the furious smoke tendrils trailing from her ears—okay, maybe I can't see it, but I do imagine it—and the sparks shooting from her eyes—also not real, but dangerously close—that she's ready to engage in one.

My happy stick jumps joyously, but the rest of me refuses to notice how wonderfully attractive Ellis becomes when she's flushed like this. Not that she's not attractive. Because she is. She's very attractive the rest of the time too. My tight balls have indicated that such a thing is indeed a fact, whether I'm aware of it in the upper regions of my gray matter or not.

"Now you've seen everything, and you know everything," Ellis hisses in the kind of tone that indicates I'm entirely responsible for seeing and knowing and also *causing*. I know she doesn't like me. I know she thinks I'm rich and spoiled. I just don't know why she has this deep and abiding dislike for me, which I can see very plainly written across her face.

"That's quite an accusation." I still refuse to rise to the fight she wants to have. Instead, I close the six-foot gap between us, and she doesn't step back. She crosses her arms over her chest, pushing up the sodden blouse she has on. It didn't dry out much in the car, even though I was blasting the AC the whole way back. The blouse is black, so it's not translucent, but it's plastered to her, and the shape of her breasts, her narrow waist, and the gentle hourglass curl of her hips are pretty obvious.

My meat stick thanks the dishwater while my eyes thank the gods.

When said eyes flick back up to her face and see how her anger is thinly veiling her absolute misery, my stomach plummets. I don't know if it's the ring or if it's just the obvious thing to do, but I open my arms and enfold them around her. She's as stiff as...well...my joystick at the moment, but let's not go there because this isn't the trashy kind of hug that comes with expectations.

"What are you doing?" she asks from against my chest. She doesn't make a move to pull away, and she doesn't lift a knee to kick me in the balls. She doesn't spit at me, literally or verbally.

"You looked like you needed a hug, so I'm giving you one."

"You're just doing it because you pity me." Yup. The voice from my chest is absolutely miserable, and it's also filled with exhaustion and vulnerability. Ellis must be seriously tired to sound like that because the Ellis I know is a spitfire. The Ellis I know doesn't do vulnerable.

"No. I don't pity you. Well, maybe just a little."

She snorts. She lifts her head at the exact moment I pull back because I'm almost certain a painful tea bagging is in my future. She tilts her head up, and her left eye twitches rapidly. Her jaw is clenched tight, but her cheeks are a lovely and delightful shade of soft petal pink, while her eyes are so dark that they're almost black.

All of a sudden, I'm reacting and listening to things I shouldn't be listening to, responding in ways I shouldn't. My hands do the work, cupping Ellis' face, and my thumbs caress the silk of her cheeks. Her eyes become wider, darker, and shocked, which I'm sure is a precursor to anger, and then I'm bringing my face to hers. I draw her close as I bring myself close. And then it happens.

Our lips meet, gently, very gently because I'm scared her mouth is like a mousetrap, and something will spring down on me very painfully and accurately, at any time.

I should stop. I should run. I feel like the mouse reaching for the cheese, getting closer and closer, and yup, almost there. Ellis' lips part and she gasps, which brings me closer to the cheese. My lips move against hers, guiding, dancing, and searching. I drop my hand away from her face and curl it around the small of her back. She melts into me in a puddle of shapely curves, hot skin, and also soaked dishwater blouse. It smells faintly of old spaghetti, and what do you know, it happens to be a turn-on.

Her lips part again, and her tongue sweeps out and tastes me tentatively. There's an explosion of light, at least behind my closed eyes, and the Ellis who hates me is suddenly replaced with an Ellis who doesn't hate me so much. Or maybe she does, but she's intent on hate-kissing. She digs one hand into my shoulder, balling up my t-shirt like it's an old rag while the other rakes through my hair, her nails scratching at my scalp while she tries to climb me like a cat. My body reacts on instinct. When my lips part, her tongue sweeps in. Her lush breasts slam up against my chest, and her pelvis bumps into mine.

I'm fully aware that this might just be a way for her to let off steam. I know the mousetrap might be hovering somewhere near the back of my neck, the cold metal bar waiting to snap, but I'm also aware that somewhere in the distance is the looming smell of cheese. Wait, no, not cheese. Christ, this metaphor has gone totally off the rails.

So have I, apparently, because now I'm dragging my tongue along Ellis' bottom lip, savoring her unique flavor. A lick isn't enough, though I would desperately like to lick her from head to toe and then back, so I suckle her bottom lip into my mouth, groaning when the sweet honey taste of her bursts over my tongue.

Her fingers brutalize my scalp, tugging at my hair. Then, her back arches, and she thrusts her breasts into my chest so hard that I can feel the hard beads of her nipples. My hand curls at her hip, grinding her into me. She mewls and squirms, butting straight into my raging erection, which kind of hurts but sends jarring white-hot heat racing through me. I sweep my hand low while I thrust my tongue into her mouth. Her jeans are tight, but they're the stretchy kind, and they cup her rounded bottom nicely. My hand fits there like it was the only thing on earth made to do it, and I squeeze her butt cheek. She hooks her leg around me and tries to climb me again, all while rocking her hips and grinding hard against me.

This is bad. This is really bad. I think we're both enjoying this, whatever it is we're doing. Maybe we're both mice, and the trap will come down on us both. I think there's a rhyme about two mice and how they meet their gruesome fate. No, wait. It was about three mice, and gruesome things happened, but they didn't die at the end, tough little bastards that they are. Clearly, my dick is draining all the blood away from my brain. I should stop thinking about mice.

Instead, I should think more about pulling away and putting a stop to this before it goes too far.

Maybe it's the curse, or the fact that Ellis grazes her teeth over my bottom lip, lets out a shuddery exhale, and attacks my mouth again. She thrusts her tongue into my mouth, stroking mine like it's a rare, tasty treasure. Her hips jam hard against my erection, and she does a wriggly dance that makes me see stars.

This curse might have fucked me over, but it's her touch that is currently incinerating me. I don't want to stop. *Do your worst, mousetrap. Do your worst, curse.*

I make one last effort to pull away, and this time, the suction of our mouths break, our hips detach, and our legs and arms untangle. Ellis takes a step back. I, however, falter back and nearly land on my ass because my legs are weak and shaky. My entire body feels weak and shaky, and I can't look away from Ellis' face, her glistening, swollen lips, and the red of her skin, irritated by the fact that it's been more than a couple of hours since my chin has seen the business end of a razor. Her blown pupils hold me captive, as do her heaving shoulders, and her breasts pushing and straining against her damp blouse with every breath. I flick my eyes up fast before she accuses me of staring at her boobs, even though I was, as they are very nice boobs.

I wonder what they'd feel like in my hands, her nipples straining under my tongue.

Christ.

Ellis' brows shoot up like she can hear my thoughts. Her

lips thin out, and a muscle in her jaw twitches as she clenches her teeth. "No. We are not going there."

"To the bedroom?" I had no plans on getting that far. I was more envisioning the couch, the coffee table—it did hold her weight during the meeting with my brother and cousins—the floor, the wall, or the ceiling. Though the ceiling is mighty high, it could be quite inventive.

"No!" She gives me a look of frosted death, and not the vanilla kind of frosting but the icy kind we rarely see down here in New Orleans. "Not to the bedroom! That just proves how far gone this is. How far wrong it is, I should say." She thrusts out her left hand. "It's this. It's making us crazy."

"I'm not sure that's all it was."

That is clearly the wrong thing to say because Ellis' nostrils flare. "I'm not interested in cursed sex, pity parties, sad sex, hungry humping—any of it."

What in the ever-loving heck is hungry humping? Maybe I'd like to find out.

"The point is, you saw what you saw, and now you feel bad for me. Poor Ellis, who lives in a dump. Poor Ellis, whose father is so depressed that he never leaves the house. Poor Ellis, who has to look after him because he can't look after himself. Poor Ellis, who is the adult and not the child. Poor Ellis, who lost her mom and is so afraid to love anything again that she doesn't even have plants or a cat. Poor Ellis, who doesn't have any close friends she can talk to about any of this, so she's slowly dying a very sad, horrible death inside while it all festers and rots, and has for years..."

Okay, wow. I'm not the only one astounded at the big speech. Ellis is pretty shocked at herself. She stops and breathes like she's being chased by a pack of wolves. Carefully, she composes her face, rearranging her features into a fuck you kind of careful mask. Then, she holds up her hand again.

"Uh, forget that last bit."

"Which bit?"

"Everything I said after the point is. It was this." She glares at the ring. "It's doing things to my tongue, making me confess things. I...I didn't exactly mean any of it."

It's my turn to cross my arms. "So you do have plants? And a cat?"

"No."

"You have some close friends you trust enough to share the hard things in your life with?"

"Not exactly."

"Your mom died?"

Her eyes automatically fill up with tears, and watching the waterworks turn on makes me feel like a complete asshat.

"A long time ago," she says, her voice wavering somewhere between *'please stop talking now because this is one subject I can't stand,'* and *'I'm ready to shut down now, so please just let me.'*

I can't do that. I can't just let what she said and what I saw tonight go, especially now that I know some of the details. "Is...is your dad...is he alright?"

Ellis doesn't know what to do about what she just told me, and I really don't know what to do about it either, so the inappropriate questions just keep rolling. The last one seems to break down whatever reserve and strength Ellis had left, but the damage is already done. Maybe this is the mousetrap I was waiting for. God, fuck the mousetrap. Why do I keep thinking about mousetraps? This is real life, and maybe this is the bit where Ellis reaches her breaking point, and shit just keeps getting real. Perhaps that kiss threw her off balance, or the cursed ring is turning her into a truth-teller. Whatever's going on, it's out there, and I'm not about to pretend I didn't hear it.

A strange surge of protectiveness washes over me. The curse? Whatever. I'm acting on it because it's what I would do for my friends, definitely what I would do for my brother and cousins, and probably what I would even do for a stranger. I might be rich, but I'm not an asshole—most of the time.

"Okay, I'm taking that as a no. Do you want to sit down and talk about it?"

Some shades of the old Ellis come back in the defiant tilt of her jaw and the stark glint of her eyes. "No."

"But you just said...I can't...I can't just ignore what you said."

"Those were facts. And here's another one. I'm not asking for your help."

This is definitely the old, spunky Ellis who likes to tell me to farge off, even if it's just with her ever-changing expressions. I swear, she has a very expressive face, and at least eighty percent of her facial muscles are used for showing disdain, shooting scathing looks my way, and betraying how much she despises me and everything related to me.

"I can help. I know people who know people, and I can find him a good therapist if that's the problem. If he needs someone to talk to."

"He has me to talk to!" Ellis snaps. I can tell I've offended and hurt her with my suggestion.

"Maybe he doesn't want to burden you with—"

"No? It's pretty clear that's what's been going on. He might not say much to me anymore in the way of actual conversation, but he says things loud and clear with the stack of dishes he never does, the house he never cleans, the clothes he never changes, the chair he never leaves, the lights he never turns on, and the TV that remains flickering and flashing constantly. He doesn't mind burdening me with that."

By the end of that very long, angry statement, Ellis has run out of steam. She visibly curls into herself, but I know she won't welcome any physical efforts I make to comfort her. I have to try again to put the offer out there, or I won't be able to forgive myself. Mental health is something that should be taken seriously, and just because someone hasn't asked or doesn't know how to ask for help doesn't mean they don't want it.

"We can't afford it," Ellis chokes before I can press on the *I want to help you* issue. "Of course I've thought about it. I've wanted him to talk to someone for a very long time."

"What if I told you I would pay for it? You could afford it then. It would be free for as long as your dad needs it and if he wants to go."

"But that's...that's..." Ellis' eyes well up with tears again, and they look like two huge stars winking in a velvet night sky.

"Please. Just ask him."

She blinks rapidly. "No. It won't do any good if I ask him. You should ask him since you know all about whatever therapist. I'm sure you think you know a little bit about everything, and you think you can fix this problem. You...you... crea... never mind. Just...fine. We'll go over to my dad's house tomorrow. And for the record, I hope he accepts your help because he needs it. I want my dad back. I want him back more than I've ever wanted anything, except maybe to have my mom back, but that's one thing you can't help me with. It's the one thing you're not resp...never mind again.

Also, for the record, I hope my dad throws a lot of things at you before he agrees to accept your help. You seem like the strong, resilient asshole type, so I know you'll stand there and take it as a matter of pride. You won't give up."

I ignore the fact that we're back to using the word asshole again. I suppose that for her, maybe there are many different types of assholes, many different categories, and maybe I fit and fall into each and every one of them. A finger there, a big toe here, a rib in that category...

But seriously, I've heard the word asshole so much that I'm starting to think I might need to change my name permanently to asshole.

"So, you think I'm strong?"

Ellis shifts from one foot to the other and drops her gaze to the ring on her left hand. "I guess we'll find out tomorrow evening. Don't worry. He won't throw the TV or his chair at you. He likes those too much. The couches are too heavy to pick up, and the coffee table is full of stuff, but I'd watch out for the lamps, though. They have weighty bases, and they're nothing special."

I do my best to hide my astonishment. "Duly noted."

"If you're done now, I guess I'll go to bed."

If I'm done? If I'm done? Oh, I'm so far from done. The next time I kiss Ellis, she won't mistake it for pity, or the curse, or hunger, or whatever she said. How could she have thought it was hunger? We ate before we left, and I don't get hungry that fast...whatever. Whatever she thought this was, I'm going to make sure that next time, she knows I'm genuine.

I'll be kissing her for her. Because she's Ellis, she's beautiful, and she's stronger than I could have ever thought possible. Because she's lonely and needs someone on her side. And because life seems to have thrown a lot of shit and asshats her way, and what she needs is a non-shitty nice hat.

Somehow, and for some reason, I want to prove to her that I'm not an asshole. Kissing her might not be the best way to go about it, but I'll worry about that later.

If the time comes.

When the time comes.

11

ELLIS

Oh, boy. I locked myself in my room this morning and worked on typing out something that passed for an article since I know my boss is going to expect something soon. At least, that's what I was supposed to be doing. I ended up just jotting down my feelings. Kind of a running journal of what's happened the past few days and an external monologue about my internal fucked-upness.

My stomach finally rumbles loud enough to send bricks crashing down around me, but still, I don't leave the spare room until Ash knocks on the door, which is sometime after lunch. After last night's massive bombshells, dropped one after the other in a fit of *what the fuck was I thinking?* I'm not surprised he's given me pretty much the whole morning to cool off. Or rather also known as coming up with a plan and getting used to the idea of him trying to talk my dad into going to a therapist.

Whatever. Maybe he didn't think about me once. It could be that he assumed if I wanted to come out, I would come out. I'm an adult and can feed and fend for myself, and Ash knows that. Maybe he locked himself in his studio, painted something horrendous, and lost track of time.

I pull open the door since this is about my dad and not me. Also, I can't stay in here forever listening to my stomach thundering like a violent summer storm.

"You ready?" Ash is wearing a t-shirt and jeans. They're regular-looking clothes, which makes him look like a regular guy.

Ha, who am I kidding? Not my ovaries or my lady cave, which feels as resoundingly empty as my stomach. If by ordinary, I meant insanely cut, then I guess Ash looks ordinary. And if by ordinary, I meant hot enough to melt globs of butter off the abs showing through his t-shirt and the biceps, triceps, delicious forearms, and veins of his arms, then yes, I suppose that would be accurate. Good, merciful god, now I'm thinking about licking melted butter off of Ash like he's a big piece of popcorn.

The scent of pine hits me full blast. Why does the guy insist on smelling like an entire store full of pine-scented air fresheners?

Jesus, someone should come in here and hose me down before I spontaneously combust. Is it possible to have an orgasm just by looking at someone? That's a stupid question. Don't answer that. What about smelling someone with a blindfold on? That would take things up a few degrees.

"Ummm, Ellis? Have you changed your mind?"

What about just hearing someone's voice?

"N...no." Ash frowns at me, and I frown back. "No, I haven't changed my mind." I remind myself that I'm doing this for my dad. The irony of the situation isn't lost on me. I should have come out last night and told Ash everything. I just about did. I almost told him that my dad's depression is his fault in the first place. But then I didn't. I just couldn't. It was like my tongue was all tied up when it should have been smooth and smooth when it should have shut the heck up. Like when I blurted out my life story.

Who tells someone they have no real friends? Ash must think I'm a real prize now. No friends, no plants, no cat, and a dad who is so depressed, he never even leaves the house. It's so abundantly clear my life went to shit after losing my mom, and I'm still not really over it the way I probably should be. Maybe Ash wants me to see a therapist too. Geez. If things keep going the way they're going, I might not refuse.

"Should I drive?" Ash asks innocently. I can tell he's trying not to upset me, to be sensitive and stuff. Right, so maybe he's not the one who's terrible at emotion.

Normally, I'd fire something snarky off, but I just nod and follow Ash out to his car. He doesn't drive at breakneck speed, and he doesn't lay on his horn. He's a nice person all the way over to my dad's house, and it's like he doesn't want to upset me and have me bail on this at the last minute. If only he knew how important this is to me. To have my dad get help. If Ash can convince my dad to see a therapist, maybe I'll admit he's not an asshole. I'd even sign a testimony stating it.

"Here we are."

As we pull up, I realize Ash remembered the directions from last night since he didn't put the address in his GPS.

I'm so nervous that I feel like I could throw up all the nothing in my stomach from not eating all day. I'm sweaty beneath the long-sleeved shirt I have on and my jeans. When you have leg sweat going on, you know you're in trouble.

"Just wait here. Let me go in first."

"Actually, I think I should go in with you. You could introduce me to your dad, and then we could talk."

"I'll exit right around the time he starts throwing lamps at you."

"Good plan. Or before that. After you let him know who I am. You could wait in the kitchen or somewhere to give us some privacy to talk. Sometimes parents won't say things when their kids are around because they want to spare them."

I roll my eyes at that. "My dad doesn't care about sparing me. You should hear the things he's told me in the past."

"Maybe this is different. Maybe he's embarrassed and wants help but doesn't know how to ask. He maybe doesn't want you to have to be responsible for him getting his act together or getting him back on track."

I could point out that my dad doesn't mind me cleaning up his messes, but I guess that's uncharitable, and it's also untrue. Dad used to protest like crazy when I'd pick up wrappers, do his laundry, or the dishes. I guess, over time, he just gave up on fighting about it with me, which is also very, very sad.

"Okay, whatever. Let's just go do this." As I spring the door handle, I realize just how terrible of an idea this might be. "Uhh...." I race to get in front of Ash, blocking the door to the house. I lower my voice to a whisper. "Don't tell my dad what your name is, okay? He won't accept any help from you if he knows who you are."

"He wouldn't recognize me anyway?"

"I...I don't know. God help you if he does."

Ash recoils. "What do you mean? What have I done? I haven't even met the man as far as I know. Have I?"

"No." At least that's not a lie. I don't think my dad has. He met Ash's Granny, yes, but not Ash himself.

"Then why would he hate me?"

"He, uh, he thinks you're a rich asshole."

Ash's right brow curls up. "Oh really? Apparently, the apple doesn't fall far from the tree. Or is this a case of the tree doesn't fall far from the apple?"

"Apples don't fall far from trees. That's a stupid saying because it's a given. And no, I suppose the tree wouldn't fall far from the apple. If the tree fell over, it would likely crush the apple. Or, if you're speaking about a future tree or trees that develop from the apple because the apple contains seeds, then I suppose it wouldn't fall at all. It would technically grow."

"I'm sorry I asked," Ash groans. "Are you sure you're actually a maid? Because I'm very sure you could make a convincing case for going and getting an English degree or something if you don't like cleaning houses."

"I, uh, yup." *Holy shit, this is way too close for freaking comfort here.* If we were playing the hot-cold game, Ash would be very, very hot. Maybe we're always playing the hot and cold game because he's always hot. Christ. I digress... "I love cleaning. You've seen me in action twice. At your house and my dad's. Can you doubt it?"

"Apples and trees..." Ash mutters. He waits for me to open the door, and we step in.

Just like last night, the blinds are closed, the curtains are drawn, the lights are off, and the only noise in the house is the TV blaring about someone who murdered their spouse. I'm really not surprised, though I'm dismayed. I get the same sinking feeling every time I walk in here. I guess I keep hoping that one day, my dad will come out of this, and he'll just be back to normal. Back to his old, driven, smart, witty self who always worked so hard for everything and cared so much about everyone around him.

I lead the way, stopping beside my dad's armchair. He doesn't even turn to acknowledge me even though he knows I'm there. Finally, I step around the chair and stand in his line of view to the TV. He raises a brow and looks at me. Then his head swivels to look at Ash. I tense, waiting for the explosive moment of recognition, but it doesn't come.

"Dad, this is a friend. A, uh, a good friend of mine. He has something he wants to talk to you about if you'll let him."

My dad blinks at me. I don't think he can believe I brought someone in here to see him like this. He must know it's beyond serious that I have. He actually grabs the remote and turns off the TV. One more long look at me, and he frowns, but not in an angry or betrayed way. Instead, he's confused and pensive.

"He was wondering, that is, he thought it might be better if you both spoke alone. I'll just be down the hall, doing laundry or cleaning the bathroom or something. If you want to throw something at him, I already gave him fair warning that you might, so feel free."

"Thanks for that," Ash mutters.

"No problem." I take myself down the hall before I can lose my nerve and do something humiliating like get down on my knees and beg my dad to accept Ash's help. Because even though it's Ash, and the help is coming from the hand I very much want to bite by publishing an awful story about, my dad needs it. We both need it. As it is, I feel like we're drowning here.

I shut myself in my dad's room. The bed is unused, which is scary. I made it up a few days ago, and he hasn't slept in it. Has he been sleeping in his chair? *Dad, please, please accept Ash's help.* Staring at the bed and the room that's clean because Dad hasn't changed his clothes in days either, a rush of moisture floods my eyes and trickles down my cheeks before I have any hope of blinking it away.

How did it come to this? I don't know if I mean my dad, me, or both of us accepting Ash's help because he's the last person I thought would ever extend a hand in kindness to us. It almost makes me want to take back the article, but then I think about the kiss. Our second kiss, actually, though the second one went way further. I was already tearing off clothes and going way too far in my mind before I managed to break away. Ash is dangerous. He's dangerous because not only am I having second thoughts about the article, but I'm having seconds thoughts about the ring and wanting to take it off. The curse must be working its cursed magic even faster than I thought.

Step one is dealing with my dad.

Step two is getting this ring off before I do a lot of things I know I'll regret.

There's a word I could use to describe Ash's kisses, which is addictive. It's a bad word. I don't know what it is about him that made me tell him things I would never in a million, billion, gazillion years just blurt out for anyone else. I know there isn't a correlation between how long you know a person and how much you trust them. You can know people for years and hardly know a darn bit about them, but I know a lot about Ash since I did some prerequisite research before applying for the maid position. However, it's no reason for me to just give him my life story as though I trust him.

It was the kiss. It did things to me, and it's like his lips were coated in truth serum. Yeah, maybe I watch too much spy shit. Probably as much as my dad watches true crime. Well, okay, not *that* much. I also love to read. Spy shit, of course. What can I say? Like my dad, I was always into investigative journalism.

All I know is, last night, I felt seen for the first time in years. I felt like Ash was looking into me and seeing things I didn't even know were there. I couldn't hide one bit of myself, so I didn't even bother, except the deceptive, nasty, snaky, snarky, betraying bits. He didn't seem to pick up on those, luckily for me.

He didn't just see me. Ash heard me.

Wait, that wasn't it. No, no, it wasn't. He heard me, he saw me, and he touched me, and I'm obviously not talking metaphorically here, though maybe he did touch those parts too.

Suddenly, *c-ccccrrassshhhhhh!*

"Aaargh!" I jump about three feet in the air and come down like a startled spooky cat, my hair bristled, back arched, claws at the ready, and eyes wild. I dash out of the bedroom. I wasn't really serious when I said my dad would throw stuff. I thought he'd contain himself. Shit. Maybe he recognized Ash, and he's now bent on revenge and is going to tear the house apart. If that's true, I have to stop him.

I enter the living room and find Ash picking up pieces of a lamp while my dad stands sheepishly beside him. "It was an accident," Dad mutters at my stupefied expression. "I got out of the chair, tripped on the cord, and pulled it off the end table."

"How did it smash on...on carpet?" The carpet is so dang plush that I think it would cushion someone from a fall of ten feet, and they'd come out of it without a scratch.

"Well, it hit the end table first, on its side, which is what caused the damage."

Ash puts the pieces back onto the wood table. "I think I got it all."

I look between them both. "Are you...are you going with him?" Dad's up. He's out of his chair. If he's not throwing things, then it must be a good sign. Actually, when I look at this face, I see something I haven't seen there in years, and my heart flutters wildly. Determination. That's what it is.

"Yes, honey, I'm going."

I let out a huge sigh of relief. Gratitude and hope also swirl around through me in a big soup pot of tenderness that makes me want to break down and turn into a big bawl bag right there on the seventies shag carpet.

I step out of the way, nodding fiercely as my eyes tear up and my throat gets wedged shut with emotion.

"We'll be back in a couple of hours," Ash says as he follows my dad to the door. I nod, still not trusting myself to say anything since it might cue up a fountain of tears I can't put a cork back on. "Will you be here?"

I nod. "Yeah," I croak. "I'll do some cleaning until you get back." I turn to my dad. There are years worth of unspoken things I need to tell him, but I settle for two words that seem to encompass it all. "Thank you."

12

ASH

It should be kind of weird and strained to be in a car with someone's dad who I barely know, and even that someone, meaning Ellis, I also can't say I know much better, but oddly, the silence isn't strained. The therapist I'm taking Ellis' dad—good heavens, we're not even on a first-name basis here—to see is a lady in her early seventies. She's been through it all as far as the field goes. She has a PhD, but she is still constantly doing case studies and research. She's taught at colleges, written more books than I can count, and done the whole office thing with clients as well. Now she works out of her house since she's semi-retired. She charges a fortune, but she's worth it.

I trust her because this is the same lady my mom saw for years after my dad left, and she really helped my mom get things back on track. It was a rough time for my mom because the divorce was brutal. I don't think she would have done as well as she did if she didn't have some good solid advice behind her. Penny Andrews was more than just a therapist. She was a friend too.

I called her late last night after my talk with Ellis. I had a list of a few other possibilities if Penny couldn't or wouldn't take Ellis' dad on short notice. I did offer to pay extra, but Penny told me it wasn't necessary or ethical to do so. She assured me she'd make room for a late appointment.

Ellis' dad shifts in the passenger seat, but he doesn't tell me he wants to bail, which is good because her office is still about twenty minutes away.

However, he does clear his throat in a dry, scratchy sort of way that makes me wish I'd had the foresight to bring some water. I feel a little parched myself. It must be the anxiety.

"How do you know my daughter?" Ellis' dad asks. "She said you're a friend, but she's never said anything about a good-looking male person being in her life before."

"If I wasn't a good-looking male person, would it make a difference?"

"You know it would, and don't give me a lecture on double standards."

"I won't." I glide through traffic easily. It's after lunch time, so it's not as heavy as it would have been one hour ago. "I...if I told you how I knew her, you wouldn't believe me."

"That's a horrifying thing for a father to hear..." he trails off and looks out the window. "But I guess I haven't been much of a father lately, as you can see."

"Actually, I think you're doing the best you can under the circumstances, which I don't fully know, and I won't presume I do, so I won't tell you how you should be acting or not acting. But I can see you love Ellis and want to protect her. When my dad left, he went to another country, pretended I didn't exist, cheated on my mom like a mad rabbit with the insane need to reproduce like it's his last day on earth, minus the reproduction part, because my father never really liked kids anyway, but you get it. Anyway, that's bad parenting. Not what you're doing."

"Maybe up in the head, your dad was the same way I was."

I shrug. "I don't really know. Things are still not great between us, but we're slowly working on it. Sometimes, he reaches out through emails, and sometimes, I email back. I'm not blaming him. I turned out alright, and we had lots going for us. But I do hold more than a mild grudge against him for how he treated my mom, though. She's a good person and didn't deserve any of it. I don't think I'll ever forgive him for what he did to her even if he came to me crawling on broken glass, walking over hot coals, and all that."

"Your honesty is commendable."

I change lanes smoothly and take a left—only fifteen more minutes. Surprisingly, I don't feel the urge to leap from the car. I feel a little bit like Ellis probably did last night—spilling my secrets without provocation—but it doesn't feel wrong.

"I do have to say I think I like you. I get the sense you would never hurt my daughter." Ellis' dad makes the same scratchy noise in his throat again. "Although, if you do, I can promise you I will tear your nuts from your body one by one —yes, it's possible—and feed them to the potbelly pig Mrs. Anderson keeps next door even though the city knows about it and has sent her no less than fourteen notices over the past two years, saying she needs to get rid of it. She's planning on hiring a lawyer because there's no way she's giving up that pig without a fight. So, the chances are good that for the next while, at least, I could make good on my threat."

I fight back a grin as that would hardly be an appropriate response at the moment. I turn toward him when we hit a red light. "I won't hurt her." I wish it were true. I want it to be true. It was never my intention to hurt anyone. I wanted to get the ring off Ellis because no one wants to walk around cursed, and it's messing with our lives, but that's as far as I planned on taking things. I'll admit there were a few little blips here and there, the kind of unexpected blip one gets when their toast gets stuck in the toaster, and they stick a knife in to try and wedge the bloody thing out, but they get more than they bargained for. Nevertheless, I still have no intention of doing Ellis any harm.

I really should stop wanting to kiss her then.

She had her hair done in a messy bun at the nape of her neck today. The clothes she wore weren't tight, but they looked amazing. I didn't know boyfriend jeans and a loose-fitting shirt could be so deliciously arousing. Bottling those thoughts and cutting my brain off from sending signals to my happy stick and happy pucks would be vital in assisting my goal of not repeating our kiss. Or kisses. Since that was the second time in which I'd kissed Ellis.

This could all end up going wrong because I want to kiss her again. And I'm always going to notice she's beautiful because she's absolutely stunning.

"I can tell you're thinking about tempting fate," Ellis' dad grumbles. "Right after I told you not to."

"I believe you warned me against hurting your daughter, which I have no intention of doing."

"Sometimes, intentions go to shit. Everyone knows that. Even the best of them."

Thank goodness we're nearly there because the urge to crawl under the dash is getting stronger and stronger. Not because I need to hide, but because I suddenly feel like I'm going to wilt. There's something about a dad giving you the stink eye that is quite withering.

"She's been through a lot," he goes on. "You don't know the half of it, no matter how well you know her. And I've been the biggest burden of all on her. I'm going to get this fixed, though I don't know why I couldn't do it on my own. I just...I couldn't. I tried. I even bought all the self-help books. She told you we couldn't afford real help, I assume?"

"Yes. She did say that."

"And you have the means to pay for it and the desire to do Ellis a solid like this, which tells me you either want to have one over her and control and manipulate her, or you're a good man with a good heart and want to do right by her. I'm going to go with the latter."

In the living room, I just broached the subject, telling him Ellis loved him and how she was extremely worried. I told him I was a good friend of hers and that I knew a great therapist who was far more human than a robot and could make a difference. I told him my mom went through a rough period when she was on her own, and she'd seen Penny for years, which helped her get through things I'm not sure she could have overcome otherwise. Then, I said the cost was not an issue and that he could see her for as long as he wanted. I also said something along the lines of how being sick sucks, and sometimes, we don't remember what it's like to feel good or even think we can feel that way again. I think he was just ready because that's all I said, and then he nodded, got out of the chair, and reached out to clap me on the shoulder, but the lamp cord got caught, causing the lamp to turn over and shatter, which brought Ellis running to us.

"I don't want to manipulate or control her."

"So, how did you both end up meeting anyway?"

"Through work." Does it sound bad? And by bad, I mean disturbingly kinky to tell her dad that she was my maid? And still kind of is? God, that's quite a mess. How could I make Ellis clean my house after this? I suppose I should find her another job instead of just kicking her out the door. That would be the first step in not being an asshole 101 and in treating her right, as her dad asked me to do.

"Work?"

"Uh, yeah." I have a feeling more questions are coming, so I cut it off. "I…we…we had to work on a project together, and it was quite intense. A strange project. More of a problem we had to solve."

"A problem?"

"It was sort of a curse."

Ellis' dad takes that oddly in stride. I pull up in front of a quaint old three-story gingerbread house in a darling neighborhood filled with ancient old mansions with turrets, wood shingles, wrap-around porches, brick, stained glass, and other bygone building materials. I haven't been here before, and I can't really believe this is the address, but well, then again, maybe I can. It kind of looks like something out of a fairy tale since it's painted pink, purple, yellow, and green. There are two turrets rising up on either side of the house, scalloped shingles, wood shutters, stained glass, bay windows on the bottom, a massive wrap-around porch, and a stone fireplace outside. Yes. Stone. Who the heck has a fireplace in New Orleans?

Anyway, this house looks more like a candy shop than a place for therapy, but that's probably a good thing. Who wants to sit on a hard leather couch and let someone pick at their brain like a rabid rooster? Certainly not me, and not anyone. The image of how therapy used to be done should just get thrown out the window. Penny has enough education and experience to know how to help people, and if she thinks this is the right atmosphere, then I'm glad.

Ellis' dad opens the passenger door, but he still has his seat belt on.

"Do you want me to come with you? Penny's expecting you. You're her last appointment, so there isn't any time limit. Please feel free to book in as many times as you would like after. You can set your appointments with her if you would like more after this one, so they're scheduled. She knows how to take care of the billing. You won't be asked anything about that."

He squints at the colorful house. "You sure this is the right place?"

"Yes."

"Does she hand out free lollies?"

"What the heck is a lolly?"

"Suckers?"

"Oh. Uh, I don't know. If you want one, I'm sure she could get one to you in short order. Or have them ready for your next appointment."

Ellis' dad huffs. "Does she have a unicorn farm in her backyard?"

"I would say chances are high, based on the look of the front of the house."

His lips twitch, and it's so like his daughter's when she's trying to hold back a smile. "Does she put extra sprinkles on already sprinkled sugar cookies after she ices them with pastel colors?"

"Chances are high."

"Good. She probably likes making the world a better place, which is a good quality to have if she's into therapy."

I nod. I could tell him all about Penny, how much education she has, how many studies she's done, all the papers and books she's published, and all the awards she's won, but I damper it down and say nothing. It's better for Ellis' dad to just go in and find out for himself.

"If it doesn't work out with her, or you don't like her or her style or whatever, I can find someone else, someone decent. Whatever you like, and in whatever atmosphere you like."

Ellis' dad turns back to me, removes his seatbelt, and hones in on my face with the sharpest, most intelligent set of eyes I've ever seen. "Why are you doing this, really?"

"Because you need it."

It's the only answer I can think of giving. I don't know how it's going to go over or how many other questions it'll raise, but I know I'll sit there and answer all of them if Ellis' dad wants to ask them. He just accepts my answer, though, likely because it's truly sincere. Maybe it means there are a few good people left in the world, and when someone tries to do something nice, people don't always have to believe they have ulterior motives. At least, I don't think I do. I'm pretty sure I don't.

This isn't a way to get into Ellis' pants or win points with her dad.

This is just because I have the money, and someone needs to do this man a good turn. Because a good turn can change everything.

"That curse?" Ellis' dad grunts as he gets out of the car. His feet hit the curb, and then he's firmly planted on the sidewalk, looking back at me.

"Yes?" I'm honestly not sure how to get into this at the moment. This isn't just a yes or no answer, and even I don't understand the semantics of it. Not like anyone would believe it anyway, which reminds me that I seriously need to talk to my granny. At this point, she is the only one who can help me out. And I seriously need help. This whole curse thing is becoming a little too dangerous, especially when I'm around Ellis. It's making me want to think unthinkable things.

"You're familiar with the saying about curses being blessings in disguise?"

I slowly work my head up and down in affirmation. I think if he knew what kind of curse we were talking about, he wouldn't see it as a blessing. In fact, I shouldn't see it as a blessing. I shouldn't be getting a strange pain in my chest when I think about finding a way to outsmart the curse, getting the ring off Ellis' finger, and going our separate ways so I can get on with my fake fiancé and fake marriage. But that was what I wanted, though, wasn't it?

"Should I call Ellis when I'm done?"

"Oh, right. Penny has my number. She'll give it to you, and you can call me. I'll pick you up. Take your time. I have a couple of errands I can run and a few calls I have to make." To my granny. To tell her there's been a disaster and to demand she lifts the curse she cursed us with because she's a badass granny who is batshit crazy.

Ellis' dad shuts the car door but then opens it again and leans in. "Remember what I said about the pig and your dingleberries."

"Yes, sir, I got that. I don't think I could forget. It's quite a graphic picture."

He just nods in satisfaction before heading up the steps of the vibrant candy-coated Victorian house. I wait to make sure he gets in, then I drive off and start making hands-free demands on my cell phone to get my granny on the line so we can get down to business and talk about the curse she so lovingly cursed us with. Gull dang meddling grannies anyway. Got to love them because what else can one do if one does not want to be doubly cursed?

13

ELLIS

My dad's house is a heck of a lot cleaner when he and Ash get back a few hours later, but I'm basically on my last limb. This house gives new meaning to bone-weary as I can literally feel the exhaustion radiating from the marrow of my bones. Maybe that's too dramatic, but try vacuuming and carpet-cleaning a shag carpet that is approximately six thousand years old with enough dust to destroy any vacuum cleaner in a matter of seconds.

The nice seventies lino is all scrubbed and glistening—if ancient orange and yellow-flowered lino can glisten—the windows are washed on the inside, because heck no, I wasn't about the tackle the outside as well. The dishes are done, all the laundry is finished, and every single bed has been laundered and remade. I probably just about broke my dad's washer, putting that large a load of curtains in at once. It made a horrific clunking sound and nearly hopped out of its confines in the laundry room. Loud bangs and clangs were all it had to say for a good twenty minutes, and then it stopped with the loudest clunk, but thankfully, it washed the next load just fine. I guess it will live to see another day.

As my dad walks through the kitchen door, I swipe back a sodden strand of hair. All of me is wet from my hair down, and unfortunately, it's not from the dish or laundry water. It's straight-up sweat. Don't fool yourself by thinking lady sweat doesn't stink the same as man sweat because I'm sure it's no better, and I probably smell like the wrong end of a cow at the moment.

My dad doesn't care as he smiles at me. Yes, he actually smiles, and that is worth its weight in gold. He rushes forward, his arms outstretched, and I rush into them. We grasp each other, hugging it out sweaty person style. Not that he's very sweaty, but more like I have enough for the both of us.

"I'm sorry, baby," he says in his deep, raspy voice. He uses this voice for when things get really emotional, and I know he's just a few steps away from breaking down, which I've only seen him do a few times in my life. It tugs at my heart and gets the tears flowing, and I soak my dad's shirt with them as he smooths my hair. "I'll keep going to the sessions and start processing through all the things I've bottled up for so long. It's my choice as to whether I want medication, but I think I'm going to hold off for a few more sessions and just get the talking part further down the road before I start with other options. I'm going to get better, and I'm going to be there for you. You don't have to be the parent anymore. You're always looking out for me."

Great. Dad's voice shifts to more of the rusty chainsaw variety, and I'm finished. We're both crying, clinging to each other, and soaking each other with sweat, tears, and maybe even a little snot. When I pull away and rub my sore, swollen eyes, I can see Ash standing in the kitchen doorway. He has his arms crossed, and he looks totally at ease there. He also has zero smugness about him. Instead, he just looks happy. Seeing his perfectly handsome face completely devoid of anything other than that one emotion does things to me. Not in a shivery, ovary-awakening way, but in a much more wholesome, deeper, and raw way one experiences when one feels a connection with someone because they've shared something meaningful.

I can't believe I'm having one of these moments with Ash Asswell. I mean Cromwell. And I shouldn't call him an ass, asshat, asshole, douche, douchebag, or any other name after this. No, he didn't save my dad as this is just the first step in a very long path, but he did reset my dad, and I guess me too, along with it. He did it for us when he didn't have to, and it means a lot to me.

"I'll let you get back to what you were doing before you had to come and scrape my ass out of that chair," Dad says. He looks a little bit embarrassed over the big display of emotion as I hug him one more time.

"Okay." I need to do a full-face swipe again to clear away the tears. "Okay, dad. I'll be back in a few—"

"No, honey, let me call you. You absolutely do not need to come and clean this house every couple of days. I've got this, and I'm not going to slide backward again. I promise I'll call you tomorrow night. And we'll set up dinner. Or lunch. Either here or out somewhere. You pick."

Before the tears start coming in great rushes again, I nod, blow my dad a kiss, and hightail it out of there. Ash opens the passenger door for me, and it's the icing on the not-asshole cake. Because assholes don't hold open doors, help complete strangers, and kiss like—*nope. We are not going there. Assholes can be good kissers.* I happen to know that for a fact from previous experiences.

We're both quiet, each of us lost in thought, or at least I am, while Ash drives us back to his house. When we pull up, there's a sleek black car in front. Even I, with my limited knowledge of cars, know it's one of those expensive beasts that came from Europe. It's also a classic. There's no way I would park it on the street, but I can see the shadow of a large form behind the wheel, and I realize that whoever this is, they're not only rich enough to afford something that came straight out of the fifties or sixties—I really am useless with my car decades—but they have a driver for it too.

"Who's here?" I point out the car, trying hard not to shiver. It seems a little bit sinister. Like maybe Ash is mixed up in things I don't want to know about. Underground things that would make a good story.

Ash's eyes twinkle, but not in the sort of way that means whoever owns the car is a gangster come to do business, or even worse, bust kneecaps. Then, he answers, "My granny."

Oh. That explains a lot. The price of the car, the driver, the classiness of it, and how it's black and looks a little bit gangster. Not that I think his granny is underground, but she sure has taken over a lot of this city and the world's media.

"She's inside?"

"Yeah. She has the code for the door."

"Of course she does." My tone indicates I'm less than thrilled to have this confrontation—oh, I mean meeting—with his granny right after a very emotionally trying evening. Plus, I'm still sweat-soaked, so I look like a bedraggled dog who bathed in its own stink. On a grossness scale of one to ten, with ten being really fucking nasty beyond redemption, I'm at least a six hundred and fifty-two.

"Hey." Ash sets his hand on my knee as we pull into the garage, and I nearly explode through the roof of the car. He retracts it quickly, and I force myself not to be so jumpy.

"Sorry. Long day."

"I, uh, I was going to say..." He kills the ignition. "That I called my granny because I thought she could offer some unique insight into the situation."

"The situation?" It just goes to show how tired I am that the ring doesn't even occur to me until I catch Ash squinting at it. "Oh, yeah. That situation."

"Maybe it wasn't the best idea to call her. I meant for her to come over tomorrow, but I should have known she'd be beside herself with granny delight. Anyway..." He shakes his head, smiling innocently enough. He looks boyish and charming, and if I weren't so gross and tired, I'd take note. And banish those notes to the fiery abyss part of my mind where all nonsense thoughts should end up. "I didn't mean for her to come right over, but she wanted to do just that."

"Good lord."

"She's not that bad."

I want to argue, but I'm all out of steam, and I have to remember that Ash just did me a very major solid, so I drag my carcass from the car and back to the house.

Where I'm promptly greeted by a five-foot ball of flying curly white hair, dazzling false teeth, about six pounds of flashy jewelry, and a black velvet ballgown. Also known as Ash's granny.

"Ooohhhh!" She shouts like she's going to enter into battle, but really, I think she's just overcome with unrestrained joy. I barely have time to get in the door before boney arms wrap around my shoulders, and a set of false teeth starts clacking in my face. "You, little missy, must be Ash's soulmate! Oh, I'm so happy this day is finally here! The first soulmate for all my cursed grandchildren! How very exciting!"

"Whaaaa...I mean, uh, I guess that's me," I say as soon as Ash's granny's arms drop away, and she allows me to catch my breath. She's grinning so wide that it looks like her false teeth could pop right out of her face and hit me smack dab in the forehead. It's probably an occupational hazard around really smiley grannies. "Except that the ring, uh... well, I put it on by accident. It doesn't make me Ash's soulmate. We don't even know each other."

His granny snorts at that. "Oh dear me, all soulmates have to meet somewhere. It doesn't mean you are, but the ring chose you for a reason."

"I'm not sure how much of the curse I believe in, but it didn't choose me. I put it on, stupidly. And now it won't come off."

"Because it chose you."

"Because it's an evil crappy object."

One stark white brow shoots up at my words. Ash's granny is seriously really pretty. She clearly likes jewelry and, uh, fancy clothes. The velvet ballgown makes her look like she's set to go to a masked ball. She has a nice, petite figure that makes her look like a little girl until you reach her face, which is still really pretty too. She's one of those women who looks gorgeous at every age. If she wasn't a Cromwell and hadn't ruined my dad's life and mine by extension, I guess I would say I hope I can look as good as she does when I'm that old.

Ash's granny is outgoing. I can tell that about her right away. She has this sort of sparkly sparkle going on that is quite intimidating for someone like me, who would rather sit in quiet with a good book. I guess I got used to shutting down, and it kind of became a trend. I don't let anyone get close to me. I know I have a problem with that.

"Granny, can you please tell us about the ring instead of just telling us that Ellis is my soulmate? We want to know the details. Like where you got it, who cursed it, can it be undone, and how it can be broken."

"Don't get your meat stick bent out of shape," Granny says casually, but I'm floored. Did she really just say something that dirty to her own grandson? "Can you get me a drink? I'm parched. All this talk of curses works up a thirst."

"We've barely started," Ash groans. "And how can you be so much older than me and still be this immature?"

"Immature?" Granny scoffs. "You think I'm immature because I use words like meat stick? Good heavens, I thought you'd be of the age where you'd have heard it being called a lot worse."

Ash becomes about ten shades paler and greener. "You're my grandma. It's just wrong."

"What's wrong is you're standing there instead of pouring me a mimosa. I have every intention of getting rip-roaring drunk while I talk about this curse. That's why I had Hancock drive me."

"Your driver's name is Hancock?" I choke out.

Granny shoots me a very satisfied look. "You bet it is. I interviewed many, many drivers until I found one with such a pleasing and entertaining last name. He doesn't mind in the least that I've cracked at least half a dozen *hundred* good jokes about it."

Ash, thoroughly disgusted now, or should I say grossed out, goes to the fridge. He actually does have a bottle of champagne and some orange juice in there. I don't know how to make a mimosa, but apparently, it's not a skill Ash lacks. Soon comes three glasses, which he starts pouring fashionably enough to rival any bartender.

Suddenly, Granny dips her head and looks at me funny. And it takes me a few rather uncomfortable seconds to realize she's *inspecting* me. "Turn around, honey. Let me get a good look at you."

This is entirely humiliating, but I comply. I spin in a fast circle, and Granny hoots. "Very good! Nice bum!" I must look every bit as offended as I feel because she asks me next, "Are you a prude?"

"Granny!" Ash snaps. "That's enough! You're not being helpful. You're being a cantankerous, nasty, nosey old lady. Plus, you're the cause of all our problems, so I wouldn't get all hot and bothered about us taking a liking to you at the moment."

"Hot and bothered?" Granny titters. "I'm not the one hot and bothered."

Ash turns scarlet from his chin all the way to his lovely, dark hair.

"Anyway, *are* you prude?"

I realize the sooner I answer, the sooner we can start talking about the curse, at least I hope, and it means I can get to bed shortly after that, which is what I truly want. Oh, and a shower, in which I will not do naughty things to myself while thinking about Ash, wishing he could—*whoa nelly, what the heck is going on with you, brain? Are you in there? Yeah, you're there, but what did you do with my good brain that didn't think foul thoughts every other second of the day? Can I please have my good brain back? Oh no! What if the curse has infected my gray matter? Shit. Shit, shit, shit, shit.*

"N...no," I stammer, just to interrupt my own panic. "No, I don't think so."

"Good." Granny appears very smug at that. "Then I can discuss dating details with you. All my grandchildren are too grossed out to imagine that love can blossom at any age."

Ash shoves his hands over his ears, proving her right.

Granny cackles. "See? Anyway, I met a guy at a gardening club last month, and we hit it off." She pumps her hips wildly, and my mouth drops open. "Too bad I don't have any cursed items to tell if he's my soulmate or not. I gave them all way to my ingrate grandchildren, who made a pact against them, which was technically a pact against love and all my hopes to see them happy. I don't understand it, really, I—"

"Granny!" Ash adds a heaping amount of champagne to one glass, pours in a splash of orange juice, and sets it down on the island in front of his grandmother.

"What? If you're going to lecture me on finding love at my age or tell me love is impossible at any age, then please take your angst-riddled person out of this kitchen. Make yourself useful and order a pizza. I'm starved. Oh, you don't want to order pizza? Well, that's too bad. I'm not talking about the curse until I get some pizza."

"I'm not ordering pizza," Ash grunts. He pulls back an entire glass of champagne and chugs that shit straight up—I don't know how because those bubbles would shoot right up the nose. "And you're going to spill everything you know about this curse because you got us into this mess, and we badly need out of it. We don't know each other, and we don't even like each other. This is all wrong. I do blame you for it, and I do think you meddle too much. I do love you, but—"

"No pizza, no talk of curses!" Granny stomps her foot. She's wearing four-inch black pumps to match her dress. I have a feeling she's going to some swanky event after this, and that's why she's dressed up. On a weeknight.

Whatever.

So, Ash's granny is winning points with me by the second. But so freaking what?

"I'm. Not. Ordering. Pizza."

"Well then..." Granny shrugs, downs her glass of champagne faster than Ash did, wipes her mouth with the back of her hand, and treats him to a grin. "Have a great night, you two lovebirds. I'm off."

With an airy wave of her hand, Granny strides off, walking like she's on the red carpet in those heels and her gown. Her elegantly curled hair swirls around her shoulders like a gauzy cloud as she leaves. Ash chases after her, but all I hear is him begging, then the door opening and closing. A few minutes later, he comes back to the kitchen, utterly defeated.

"Holy shit, what just happened?" He looks like a crazy storm just rolled over him, and I think I must look the same too.

"Granny. Granny just happened. Now you can fully appreciate how potent the curse is."

"Uh, yeah. I think I can." I walk over, drink the one remaining mimosa in a few sips because I'm not as talented at chugging it back as the Cromwells are, and head out of the kitchen. "I need a shower. And to go to bed. Goodnight, Ash. Thank you for all your help today with my dad."

"But not with the curse."

I have to hide my grin by turning my face away. "No. Not with the curse." I can't let him see that I actually liked his granny. And I don't want him to know that I might be softening when it comes to him too. Bad things come from being soft and letting people in. I mean, not always, but it would be bad if I went all soft and gooey and let Ash in. In both a figurative and literal way.

14

ASH

I try desperately to ignore the sounds of the shower. Actually, I know I can't hear anything at all because the house is literally built like a brick shithouse, and it's well insulated and just about fully soundproof from one room to the next, and certainly from one floor to the next.

So, no, I most certainly *cannot* hear the shower. I *cannot* hear the water running, sluicing off Ellis' delicious curves, hitting the drain, and disappearing. I *cannot* hear her fingers in her hair, massaging in the shampoo and washing it away before working in the conditioner. I *cannot* hear her using the body wash—my body wash. And I definitely *cannot* hear her hands sliding over her body, working magic—I mean working the soap over her tired muscles.

But I *can* imagine it.

I really shouldn't blame the curse, but well, I think I'll blame the curse. I also think that instead of standing around the kitchen and pacing the living room, I need to go upstairs, get changed into proper workout clothes, and banish myself to the basement for a good few hours before I hit a shower of my own. And uh, not work my magic.

Just work in the soap. I'm pretty sure no amount of rubbing one out is going to help with the ache in my balls. Maybe I'll also blame the curse for that. Damn, damn curse.

And damn my damnable granny for refusing to tell me a thing about it. Maybe she doesn't know, and she's just being her regular granny self. Or it could be that she wants this to work out. Perhaps she's also tupping her driver. The grin on his face when I walked by earlier was totally unnatural. *Christ, Granny.* I love the woman to death, but she might seriously be the death of me and my cursed ass one day.

I head upstairs, taking them three at a time, already getting my workout in. They're metal and quite narrow. I could probably try four at once. You know, if I want to land on my face, which might actually distract me from my abominably aching erection. The moment I get to the top of the stairs, I hear a door creak. I freeze like I'm wearing all black and have a crowbar in my hand, all set to break into my own house.

The curse might be one of those time-shifting bastards because everything seems to stop. I can hear the first muted footstep on the hardwood floor—Ellis' footstep. I remain frozen, as frozen as I was when the ring box went bouncing down the stairs, straight to her, and when she slipped it onto her finger and started this whole thing.

She walks out, and I'm expecting to see her wearing pajamas of some sort, her hair sleek and dripping at the ends, but no because that would be too easy. Too easy on me, and too easy on the Abominable Dick in my pants. Instead, Ellis is wearing nothing but a fluffy black bath towel. *My* fluffy black bath towel. And she does indeed smell woodsy and spicy. Like my body wash. My shampoo is more floral, and yes, I'm manly enough to admit that I like the scent. My mom bought it for me once, and I liked it, so I kept buying it after.

The black towel is big enough to wrap around her body three times, which only makes me realize how small she is compared to me. It hides all her curves, thank goodness for small mercies, but she has it wrapped low on her chest. So low that if it slipped an inch, it might reveal the dark shade of her areolas.

Now my dick is more like the Abominable Raging Inferno.

"Garg!" Ellis yelps when she sees me. She doesn't have the towel knotted, just tucked under her arms, and it slips about a fraction of an inch. I gasp. She gasps. And I remain frozen, in the *just freshly caught are you going to call the police* burglar pose. "Shit," she says. "I left my clothes in the bedroom. I always do that. I was just walking there now. To, uh, change."

"Right. Yes. I was just walking to my room to change as well. To go work out. In the basement."

"I...right. I'll just walk around you then."

I step forward even though my dick is severely impeding my ability to walk. It's a thing. Trust me. It's a real thing. "Right. Me too."

We each have to go the other way, past each other. The hall is wide. Like wide enough to fit a bus and then some. Okay, maybe not that wide, but it's wide enough for us to stick to our own lanes and pass cleanly without a head-on collision.

Except that's precisely what happens. We each start heading in the right direction, but then all of a sudden, things come to a head, and we're facing each other. I go to dodge left, and she dodges right, which is my left and her right, and we nearly step right into each other. We both chuckle an embarrassed laugh and step in the opposite direction, right into each other's path again.

"Okay. I'll go left. You go right." It sounds like a solid plan when it leaves my mouth, but I guess I forgot that my left is her right.

So, we both step. Together. And bam.

The head-on collision I thought could be avoided hasn't been avoided at all. It happens with a bump, then a bang. Elbows and knees, lips and teeth...and what? Why am I suddenly bracing Ellis' arm with my hand, bracketing her cheek with the other, and tugging her closer than she already is? Why is she leaning into me, her face tilted up, her lips parting, and meeting mine? Why am I kissing her so eagerly that our teeth clash just a little before we finally get our faces at the right angle, which I assume is both our right, but who knows because so far, I've made a mess of trying to give directions, and our tongues get the right-right, the left-left, and the right-left? They clash, too, although that clashing is more of a pleasant war.

"Oh god," Ellis pants. "This is really bad."

"It's the curse."

"The curse of the curse. Now it's making it so we can't avoid each other. Wait, are you...why are you grinning like that?"

My stomach constricts, and the blood leaves my brain, rushing south of the border. Am I grinning? No. I'm not grinning. She's grinning. Well, I guess that's not really how it goes.

"You're smiling so hard that you have dimples. Oh my god!" Ellis clutches at her towel. "Holy crap. You never showed those off before. Now you're bringing out the big guns, and how am I supposed to resist a charming smile with dimples?" She hikes her towel, pulling it up under her armpits and folding her arms tightly over the top. She's utterly adorable, and all I want to do is take her in my arms —towel and all, though it would be more fun without it— and kiss her until she can't breathe.

"Are you saying my smile is charming?"

"Argh! When you want to be, I'm sure you can be." Then, she frowns. "Now, you go this way, and I'll go that way." She points, and her towel slips an inch. My mouth goes dry, and I think I just felt my dimples deepen.

"Alright."

"Okay. One, two, three." We step together and end up walking right into each other again.

"Oh, for the love of farge," Ellis curses. Her arms wrap around my neck, mine slip around her waist, and the towel gets jammed between us. "Why fight it?"

Her breasts are pressed into my chest, and her nipples are so hard that they're cutting through the towel and my t-shirt. I might be hard enough in other parts too. Maybe my nipples, boy berries, and boy-stick joystick, or perhaps all three. Or, well, technically five if we're counting individually here. Her hips wriggle beneath the towel, and I know she can feel all the hard bits.

My heart pounds as hard as my dick, which is saying a lot as there happens to be a lot of blood surging in that direction. I stare into Ellis' face, waiting for her to retract the last statement, but her full lips open in invitation, and shit, she's right. We're both directionally challenged and cursed. How can we stand up against that? This really isn't our fault.

Ellis is complicated, but I mean, I am too. Everyone is. What I mean to say is she astounds me. She's equal parts firecracker, sassy, mouthy, loving, and gentle.

"If I kiss you, is it going to make you want to run the other direction?"

She rolls her eyes. "I'm not the one who is love challenged here."

"Love challenged?"

"You had a pact against falling in love."

"It was to prevent the curse and I didn't— don't believe in the forever love bullshit."

"Yeah, well..."

"Am I going to scare you off if we do this?"

"Define this."

I groan. She throws her head back and laughs, and honestly, the sound is so beautiful that I can't begrudge her one bit. "I'm not running. Just so you know."

"It's kind of hard to run when you're cursed to be together."

I bend my head and kiss the curve of Ellis' neck. Her skin is still damp from her wet hair, and a volley of goosebumps blossom on her skin when my lips meet that sensitive place. She doesn't pull away, and I don't know if it is me or us or the curse, but I want to do more. Ellis starts trembling when I rain kisses over the beautiful curl of her shoulder. She has extremely nice shoulders, and she's flawless, her skin pale and creamy. She's slightly cold against my lips, which is a wonderful contrast since I feel like I'm on fire.

Now my cock isn't just aching as my balls are booming. Like cannonballs.

"If I scoop you up in my arms and take you to my room, would you run?"

"Where would I run to?" Her sigh is meant to be sarcastic, but it comes out in a way that makes my cannonballs feel like they're going to blow me to bits.

I look her in the eyes this time, and she meets my gaze, challenging me with every bit as much intensity as I feel. "If I took you to my room, would you—"

"Or for the love of pity peter pumpkin patch, just kiss me already."

She wraps her hands around my neck again and pulls me into her. Our mouths meet, and I devour every bit of her mouth like she's the candy store, and I'm the kid with zero self-control. I grasp her around the waist, but she jumps, so my intention of swinging her up like a damsel-in-distress is entirely thwarted. She wraps her legs around my hips, and holy sweet sugary shucks, her core is sans panties, sans towel, sans anything. I can feel her heat through my jeans, which is a dangerous thing when I'm already next to just about zero control.

Ellis attacks my mouth and tugs at my hair so hard that my scalp nearly ignites. My entire body feels heavy with need.

"Bedroom," Ellis rasps against my mouth. "Now!"

It's a pretty clear directive, and what do you know, I'm suddenly not directionally challenged at all. I get there just fine, clearing the door even while her tongue is in my mouth and my brain is going haywire.

My king-sized bed is waiting like a divan made for a queen. I mean to set Ellis on it gently, but as soon as I'm halfway across the room, she scrabbles against me and tears her mouth from mine.

"Set me down," she demands.

My arms obey, quite literally, and she nearly drops on her bottom. It's a good thing I catch her halfway down. She lets out a grunt but doesn't miss a beat. Her towel drops, and I'm so stunned by the sight of her glorious curves, perfect breasts, flat belly, curvy hips, and sleek legs—yeah, I do notice all that and not just the obvious spots—that I miss her hands moving until they're tugging the hem of my shirt.

"Take it off," she commands. "I want to admire and stare at all your man muscles."

I gulp. She grapples with my shirt, and I have to help her when it gets lodged at my shoulders. I scrabble at it, too, my fingers barely working. The shirt gets stuck halfway up my face, gives my nose a good tug, and stings against my eyes and forehead. With a grunt, I lift my arms, freeing myself from the cloying contraption.

"Ahhhh," Ellis sighs when it hits the floor somewhere behind me. "That's much better."

"So you admit you like it?"

"Yes, I'll admit it. When did I say I didn't?" She puts her hands to her hips, and since she's standing there naked, I can't help but think it looks incredibly comical, and I have to struggle not to grin.

Grinning would make me seem smug, and I don't want to appear that way. There's plenty of time for that after I strip my jeans off.

"I said I didn't like you," she clarifies. "I even said you were an asshole and that your art sucked. But I never said you weren't all muscly and full of dimples. Wait! Turn around!" Her tone is so commanding that I just do it without thinking. "Ooooh!" she sighs. "You have butt dimples too."

"What the heck are butt dimples?"

"The things above your butt. Those two indents. They're very nice on you."

"Should I take off my jeans so you can appraise the rest of me?" I ask with a laugh.

I swear Ellis' pupils grow to twice their size. "Yes," she grunts thickly. "You definitely should."

This might be the strangest way I've ever undressed in front of someone, but it's also kind of hot. Well, okay, it's super hot. Who doesn't like to take commands from a beautiful, sexy, naked woman who is getting more and more turned on with every bit of clothing I strip off?

I go slowly, unbuttoning my jeans, unzipping them, and never taking my eyes off Ellis. She also never takes hers off me, and they widen when I pull my jeans and boxers down. I try to make it seem like a confident, fluid motion, but then I kind of miss when I try to step out of the one pant leg and end up pitching forward. My leg is still in the other as well, so I pitch off to the side when I try and right myself.

"Gaaahh!" The floor comes up fast, but I manage to break my fall by ending up on my ass.

"Hmm," Ellis sighs. "That was incredibly romantic." She walks over, kneels in front of me— yes, kneels in front of me —and starts stripping off my jeans. They're caught inside out, and she has to tug hard even though they're not tight. Eventually, she strips them off and stares at me. It would be disconcerting if her eyes weren't all smoky, her lips weren't parted, and she wasn't looking at me with a shit ton of obvious desire.

"Wow," she breathes. It's a nice compliment, especially given the somewhat less than graceful way I came to sit on the floor.

Usually, the guy is supposed to take the lead, I mean, that's just the chivalrous thing to do, but when Ellis' small hands trail up my legs and end up on my knees, I'm just fine with taking orders—letting her work her magic and have her way with me.

I'm more than fine when she pushes my legs down to the floor and kneels over me. My dick is so hard that I'm literally looking the bastard right in the face, which means Ellis can lower herself down without a bunch of things happening when she does. Yeah, my penis is already that erect. And we are still at what I'd classify as the foreplay step. I think.

God, I want to be on that step.

I realize I'm breathing too fast, and I'm just sitting here, staring at Ellis, but her boobs happen to be really close to my face, and they're incredibly luscious with the most perfect, dark, little peaked nipples. She makes a sound in her throat that I take as permission, and I bring my head forward while her hands settle on my shoulders. I palm her breast, guiding her to me, and suckle one of her nipples into my mouth. She groans, her nails grip my shoulder, and her hips sink a few inches.

It's a miracle my balls don't explode. It really is. Somehow, she managed to turn something very unsexy—me falling on my ass—into something pretty freaking wonderful, which is me getting to taste her delicious, honey-drenched nipples, feeling her sleek legs around my hips, and the delightful heat radiating out from between her legs. She's so wet that when she sits down on me and grinds against my leg, I can feel all the moisture pooling on my overheated skin.

"God, can I taste you?" I fully expect the answer to be something snarky about how I already am, given that I just had her nipple in my mouth. I draw it back in, teasing, suckling, and rolling my tongue over the tight bud before I pull back. Then, I blow a breath of cool air over it, just so I can watch her shiver and tighten and get even harder.

"Mhmm," Ellis pants. "How?"

I'm honestly a little shy about putting it out there, so I wrap my hand around her hips and guide her core up my chest. Ellis lets out a squeak of surprise, but her hands hit the floor easily above my head, and she positions herself over me without hesitation. If this is the last view I ever have before I die, then I will die the happiest man on the planet.

"I know what you're thinking," she groans, but she lowers herself to my face anyway.

"Well, I'm thinking you're perfect and beautiful, and I'll probably die from the first taste because you are exquisite."

She makes a noise that is half an annoyed sigh and half a grunt, all tinged with embarrassment and a little bit of pleasure too. She's trying to hide the latter, I can tell. "And if you die, then you'll die happy. I hope that's what you were thinking."

"We're on the same page exactly. Now, will you ride my face?"

"Will you stop talking and eat me?"

Touché. Yes. Yes, I will. I run my hands over her thighs—which have broken out into goosebumps—and guide her to me as I part her folds and open her up. The first taste of her is indeed exquisite. She's so wet, and I slowly savor every single drop of her arousal.

Riding someone's face isn't exactly noise-free, but she doesn't seem embarrassed by how loudly I'm enjoying myself. In fact, her whimpers start to come in time with my moans, and her hips swivel wildly. She takes full advantage of my tongue as I explore her, part her, lap at her arousal, and eventually plunge inside her tight, slick channel.

"Oh my god," she pants. "You should not be that good with your tongue. Actually, yes, yes, you should. But...oh! Oh, oohhhhhh, uh...wow!"

I think that means I'm doing this right. Her hips roll hard into my face, and she rides my mouth, guiding me to where she wants me. She's not shy about how eager she is or how much she enjoys it, and that's hotter than anything I could have ever dreamed.

If this is the curse, then...just...wow. Like what Ellis said a few seconds ago.

"God...Ash, can I...can I come on your face?" she pants breathlessly as her hips ride my mouth hard. I slip my tongue back inside her before she rocks against me, and I dance over her folds and circle her clit. My hands grip her waist, guiding her gently, but it's mostly all her setting the rhythm.

"Yes, please. I wish you would." I can't believe I just said that, but I'm not worried about it sounding lame. I guess what I really can't believe is that we're here doing this, and it's happening already. I have every intention of slowing things down after this. If we're going to be cursed, we might as well make the most of it. Make it memorable. Take our sweet time with it.

Ellis starts writhing above me, swaying to a tune only she can hear, but man, it must be a great one. Spontaneous classical music bursts in my head at about the same time the light show starts behind my closed eyes. I wonder if she knows it's quite possible I'm enjoying this more than she is. Okay, maybe an equal amount because she's pretty into it, and it's super, super hot.

I love how we're naked, and Ellis has her head thrown back, which I can feel more than I can see. I also love how her breathing is ragged, and she's panting and writhing all over the place, shamelessly soaking my chin, cheeks, and mouth. And I especially love the taste of her, which is both sweet and spicy.

She rocks against my face, gyrating her hips in a perfect rhythm. I do my best to give her what she needs, but she also does her best to make it easy for me. Sometimes it takes a lifetime to find the perfect rhythm with someone, and sometimes it's just instant.

"Do you have any idea how hot you are?" I choked out while she's rocking hard against my tongue.

"No," Ellis giggles. "Not at all. But yes...keep...mmm, yeah. Right there! Yes, sweet nectarines, just like that. With your tongue. Right. There."

Her commands are easy to follow, so even my addled brain can understand and comply.

"Oh god," she whispers, and then she's gone.

Her pussy clenches around my tongue while she rocks and sways gently above me, riding out the waves with soft little gasps. I like that she doesn't scream or yell or shout my name. I like how, for the most part, she hardly makes a sound at all. If she had screamed my name, it would have been okay too, but somehow, those soft whimpers and gasps are so over the top sexy that I have to think about my granny doing what she always does—being horribly inappropriate and dropping nasty details of her sex life—just to keep myself in line.

Having an intimate experience where you come together is one thing, but this would not be it because this would be me blowing my load about eight years too early. So, I roughly tell my dick that it's not his turn yet. Unfortunately, my dick doesn't like to listen and take commands from my brain. Instead, my dick gives me the facts and tells me there is a wonderful, beautiful, sensual, and fearless woman riding out the aftershocks of her climax on my face with my tongue thrust up inside her, her inner muscles clenching all around it while she soaks my face.

Yeah, it's kind of hard to argue with that. I see the bastard's point.

"Holy sweet peaches," Ellis whispers above me.

"I agree," I whisper back.

She slowly wriggles off me, and I guide her down to me

gently, so she's straddling my chest. She leans in with a sigh, kisses me deeply, and rolls her tongue over my lips, tasting and savoring herself on me. She coaxes my mouth open and thrusts her tongue in, stroking mine hotly.

I go back to thinking thoughts about my grandmother before embarrassing things happen with my two biscuits and sausage. *Oh, how breakfast of you.* That, ladies and gentlemen, is the sound of my dick mocking my futile attempts to control it.

Ellis grazes her teeth on my bottom lip before she sucks it into her mouth and licks away the sting.

Oh, god, I'm definitely breakfasted now.

"What can I do for you?" she rasps. Then, she smiles coyly at me, and I'm so nearly finished that I can't think of a single thing to say.

Without waiting for me to answer, she shifts down and very neatly wraps her small palm around the shaft of my dick. I'm still speechless. She moves her hand up and down in a slow, tantalizing motion, and I realize she wasn't the only one who was extremely wet.

"Is this okay?"

Maybe, at this point, I look like I'm dying. Do I look all pinched and pruney? It would be embarrassing to give off vibes of me not enjoying this. Her hand works me slowly, and when she looks up at me, all I can do is blurt out one word.

"Breakfast!"

15

ELLIS

I'm not sure what breakfast means. Maybe it's his safe word. A code word? Something dirty I haven't heard of? "If you're hungry, I can—"

"No!" Ash leans back, and his head hits the floor with a loud thud that had to have hurt. He groans, and I gasp.

"Are you okay?"

"I...yes. Yes, I might die of mortification, but I'll survive."

I run my hand slowly over his shaft. He's quite impressively built as I can barely wrap my hand around him. But I love watching him throb, and I love watching the beads of moisture leak from his swollen tip. I also love seeing how I can make him feel like this.

"What do you mean mortification?"

"I...just...that..."

I stroke my hand slowly over the shaft again, circling the tip with my wrist and running my thumb over it to gather the droplets of moisture there before I just concentrate on it. Ash grinds his teeth. Loudly.

"Oh, I see."

"Yeah, I...can we do a dummy round?"

"A dummy round? You want to play cards now?" I keep massaging him, and his whole body trembles with his effort to stay under control. I'd like to see what happens when he loses control because it would be pretty awesome. I mean, maybe not as awesome as what I just got to do, which I still can't believe I did, because generally, I'm pretty shy, but it would be right up there for sure.

I don't stop stroking him. I keep working his dick, and then with my other hand, I give his balls a special tickle, which is really more of a slow grab and roll motion.

Ash makes a sound like he had his mouth open, a mouse came by and got curious, things happened, one thing led to another, and he ended up swallowing it.

"G...god," Ash chokes. "What do you think you're doing? That is not taking it slow."

"I didn't realize we were supposed to. Is that what a dummy round means?"

"A d...dummy round means...argh, I can't think while you've got my balls in your hand like that."

I concentrate instead on running my hand up and down the very long length of his shaft. He's equally as long as he is thick. Well, I mean, no, not equal, but you know, equally as impressive. I lower myself so that my mouth is just inches away from his dick, and Ash starts sputtering.

"A dummy round is a round where we get the first one out of the way. I...this is...yeah. It's just I...yeah."

"Oh. You're worried about coming fast. About as fast as I came on your face?"

"Umpph!" he murmurs. "Something like that."

I flick my tongue out and taste the drops of precum at the tip of his dick. They're salty and delicious. My pussy clenches hard, and a rush of wetness trickles down my thighs. I feel empty inside, achy. I might have just had one killer climax—yes, on top of Ash's face, no less—but it doesn't mean I wouldn't like another.

I'm normally not like this. Not bold, not needy, and also, things generally don't ache like this. My experience of sex has been more of the bland variety, where halfway through, I start wishing I declined the invitation and treated myself to some me-time instead, which is usually about five minutes long from start to finish. It always involves my fingers only, nothing more adventurous. Also, I never confide these things to friends. I mean, I do have some friends, but I have no best friend that I go into details with about these things, but I know if I did, they'd tell me I have a very sad, lacking sex life. It's just that I was always busy. My journalism classes were challenging and demanding. In high school, I was too busy dealing with the fallout of my mom passing away, what it did to me, and how it changed my family dynamic to worry about messing around and being a regular teenager. In college, as I said, I was just busy. I've never been overly adventurous between the sheets, and I was a journalism major, not a freaking science major, so I left the experimenting to other people.

"You're thinking about something now. I really hope it bodes well for my dick because you have a strange expression on your face. You're either concentrating or plotting something diabolical."

"Would diabolical be so bad?" I wink at Ash. I have no idea who just jumped into my body and replaced the real me because this is so unlike me. Then, I get a glimpse of my hand with *the* ring, which is curled around Ash's shaft. Oh, yeah. Right. The curse.

If this is cursed sex, maybe I don't ever want to go back to being uncursed.

"So, a dummy round. Okay." I lean forward and let my

tongue curl around Ash's cock. His hips rock forward, gently pushing his erection between my lips. He draws back after, coughing out an apologetic cough.

Now that I've had a taste, I want more, which surprises me because I'm honestly not one of those girls who like doing this. In fact, I've never really seen the attraction of oral. I'm certainly not someone who would climb onto someone's face and ask, out loud, if it was okay to come there, but apparently, I am now one of those people.

Thank you, curse.

I love the salty, manly taste of him on my tongue, and I love how my jaw aches when I open my mouth wide enough to take him. I have no illusions that I'm going to get him to the back of my throat or do anything dirty like that. For one, his dick is like fourteen feet long, so not going to happen. But I do what I can, using my mouth and tongue, wrapping my hand around the rest of him, and pumping in time to his gentle thrusts.

"God..." he groans. "This is going to...this is not what I had in mind for a dummy round."

For obvious reasons, I say nothing. Instead, I keep going, working his dick, and I think my hips might be pumping in time with his now. In my mind, they are, since the ache between my legs is so furious that it feels like my ovaries are in my throat, and my lady cave is trying to turn completely inside out.

Ash's hands tangle in my hair, but he doesn't slam my face into him or thrust brutally into my mouth. He's nice about it, guiding me gently, and I take as much as I can before I pull back. I let my tongue stroke and caress him.

"This is...I'm not going to do this," Ash protests. "You don't want me to do that."

I pull back, using my hand to keep up the rhythm. Ash's

head falls back, and he lets out another long moan. "Don't I?" I murmur.

"I…no. I can't do that. Maybe next time." He guides my face away, and suddenly, he's all coordinated again.

He scoops me off the floor and onto the bed. I land on my back, and he lands on top of me. He quickly catches himself—so he doesn't turn me into a human pancake—and kisses me hard. I can still taste myself on him, and when his tongue thrusts between my lips, I know he can probably taste himself on me. I'm already wrapping one leg around his tight, hard hip and iron-clad buttocks, opening myself as I wriggle fiercely against him. His erection digs into my stomach, and I can feel how wet he is, pooling there on my belly. I can also feel how wet I am, pooling much lower.

"Okay, get the dummy round over with. How many were you thinking after that? Just so I can mentally prepare myself."

"I…possibly at least six."

"At least six?" My head feels dizzy just thinking about it.

This is not going to be my typical experience. I'm not going to have to fake anything, let my mind drift, or try to imagine something dirty in order to produce an orgasm so that noble intentions can be satisfied. I don't have to count cats in my head—some people count sheep, but I count cats—and I don't have to think about some awkward way to make an escape after, or even worse, how to tell the other person that I don't want them to fall asleep in my bed. This is why I don't do these things often. Because it's just a pain in the ass.

But *this* is not a pain in the ass. My level of need has ratcheted up somewhere into the level of *if this doesn't happen soon, I'm going to lose my shit for real, grow to the size of some epic monster, rise up and crush buildings like they're made of cardboard while people are little tiny ants, be annoyed by harmless missiles fired from helicopters, and then go on to total world destruction with a single stomp of my monstrous foot.*

"Ash, please..." Holy shit, is that wanton, panting voice seriously coming from me? Am I really moaning his name, begging him to fuck me?

My lady cave says no amount of groveling is too much right now, and my ovaries agree. My breasts are so heavy that they might start crushing things with a single blow, and the emptiness inside me feels equally as heavy and hard to bear.

"Should I get a condom?"

"I'm on the pill. Better safe than sorry." Then, I squeeze my eyes shut because wtf kind of thing to say is that? Better safe than sorry? Meaning I don't do this often, but when I do, I want to be doubly protected. Anyone else always gets the condom talk from me. But Ash, though?

It's the curse.

The curse doesn't want anything between us.

"Are you sure? Because it really sounds like you'd prefer if I wear one."

"No. I didn't mean...I'm fine. If you're sure you're fine...I mean good...I mean..."

He looks down at me, and his eyes become all soft and thoughtful. "I actually haven't done this with anyone in a good long while. You?"

I can feel myself going scarlet. "I haven't either. I mean, I've been busy, and I've had work to think about. My dad..."

His thumb brushes over my lips, and he smiles at me so softly to match his eyes. "I'm not going to pretend I'm a player or a stud. I've only dated casually in the past because I don't do relationships or connections. I'm sorry to say it like that, but it was a mutual experience."

"And that doesn't make you a player?"

"I hope not." He swallows so loudly that it seems to echo through the room. "I know people have this perception of me, but it was mostly from when I was younger. I smartened up a long time ago and started focusing on other things. I haven't...that is...I might be a little rusty. I...good god, this is embarrassing. I haven't had any sort of practice in somewhere around six months."

Did I accuse him of being a player? Did I think it in my head, or did I say it out loud? I can't remember now, but hearing him tell me all that is endearing in the strangest sort of way. It's kind of cute, actually, how embarrassed he is.

"I have you beat," I assure him. "Well then, the dummy round. Should we resume getting it out of the way?"

He smiles at me, and those dimples of his become evident again. How did I never notice them before? I think I might have seen one appear a few times, but I totally disregarded it, probably as a self-coping method to keep my internal organs safe. All of them, not just the ones involved in spontaneous ovulation.

"Yes. Yes, we should resume it."

I grip Ash's shoulders, watching in fascination how all of his muscles ripple as he moves above me. He fits himself to me and pauses there. I wrap my other leg around his hip, urging him forward. I've turned myself into a human monkey or a crab or something, but for once, I'm not worried about whether I look okay in this position or if something might be bulging weird or squishing funny.

Ash stretches me wide with his first thrust. It's painful, and at first, all I feel is the shock of it, but by thrust number two, I'm already on board with this. By thrust three, I wonder how I ever lived my whole life without knowing this was possible. We fit perfectly. There's a lot of wriggling and shifting on my end, but by the fourth thrust, I know beyond a doubt that it's perfect.

By thrust five, I stop counting thrusts. I close my eyes and savor the sensation of being stretched wide open and filled so fully. Ash hits spots I didn't know were in my own body, and I keep wriggling and squirming against him, urging him to discover and hit more spots. I pant and make little mewling noises, and when Ash's mouth finds mine and claims those, I surrender them readily.

I arch my hips, angling to make it possible to take him even deeper. He thrusts hard, changing up the intensity. Our bodies slap together nosily, but even that is sexy and not something to cringe at and file away for later study in mortification.

"You're so tight," Ash groans.

I dig my nails into his shoulders just to hold on. "I think you're supposed to tell me that right off the bat."

"Maybe, but it's just as hot now."

He thrust again, filling me to the full, and I have to admit he's right. We're a good fit. A perfect fit. I crack an eye to watch Ash above me. He's so hot. I love that he's totally out of control, and his face is a mash of pleasure, desire, and concentration.

"So beautiful," he mutters without looking at me. I'm looking right at him, so I know his eyes are closed. "So amazingly perfect."

"So cursed," I add out of nowhere, and Ash smiles so hard with his eyes still closed that his dimples appear again.

"So cursed." It seems like the right thing to say. An agreement of sorts. Giving each other, one to the other.

I close my eyes again on the next thrust, which is harder and deeper still. We get lost in that, in each other, and honestly, I'm not sure this is a dummy round because Ash holds out longer than I do. There is no stopping the climax that bursts over me like a dam breaking and raining down beavers and sticks, and what else does a dam usually include? Anyway, whatever it's raining down, it feels white-hot and utterly amazing, and I am just so lost. So, so lost. And so, so cursed.

I feel like we're truly connected. Not just our bodies, but maybe, just for a second, our cursed hearts too. That maybe, just maybe, the ring didn't get it wrong.

I excuse that immediately as a haywire thought brought on by the flashing and bright lights behind my eyes, the waves of pleasure rocking and crashing over me, and the brain spams that match the spasms of my lady cave.

My heartbeat pounds so loudly that I can literally hear it. The waves are hotter and longer, and they drag me under and toss me around, which is perfectly fine. I'm okay to surrender to it.

And then Ash buries himself deep inside me, and I feel him tremble. He makes a grunting, caveman sort of noise so hot that it nearly sends me into another series of waves. The existing ones pick up when I know he's coming, falling apart like I am. I wrap my arms around his neck, and I imagine I'm holding him when I'm probably just holding on. He's big and heavy on top of me, covering every bit of me, and I'm enfolded in the circle of his arms. I have my legs wrapped around him, pulling him close, keeping him inside me. We're hot and sticky, stuck together in parts, soaking wet, and still, the waves keep washing over me.

This has to be the longest, most intense climax in the history of climaxes ever felt by anyone in the world and throughout history, ever.

"Holy baked potatoes," Ash grunts.

"Yeah. Loaded with sour cream and bacon bits," I pant.

"And those chive things."

"And maybe some grated cheese."

"Loads of grated cheese, topped with chili," Ash adds breathlessly.

"Chili is good," I giggle.

He kisses my forehead, grunts like a caveman again—why is that so hot anyway—and rolls to the side. My legs are still locked around his waist, so I roll with him, trembling as the aftershocks hit. I untangle myself carefully and try to regulate my breathing. Ash seems to be doing the same. I have the urge to thank him for the most spectacular experience of my life, but instead, I kiss him and let him wrap his arm around me as I rearrange myself next to him. I tuck my head against his damp chest, inhaling the delicious and dark male aroma that comes off of him in heady waves. He's spicy and salty, and god, was there ever a better combination? Don't get me going on sweet and salty because I'm still hoping that's coming.

"So, if that was the dummy round, I'm curious about the others."

Ash runs a hand over my hair, and I practically melt because it feels so intimate with his heart hammering under my cheek. "Soon. Unless you want to kill me, I promise, soon."

"Oh. You're going to do the thing all guys do and fall asleep now?"

I can already hear his breaths getting deeper, and somehow, even that is intimate and touching. "I'm just going to rest my eyes. I need five to recover from the dummy round, and then you'll have the real thing."

My lady cave throbs in excitement though I don't know how because she was just truly and thoroughly pleasured twice. There are things I clearly don't know about my own bits. Like how right they feel with Ash's bits and how much they enjoy the shared experience between us.

I realize then, with no small amount of horrible shock, that I'm truly, irrevocably, and beyond a doubt—*I don't know anymore if it's just about the curse*—entirely screwed.

This Ash isn't the Ash I thought he was, and I've completely changed how I feel about him. I have to break the curse before I spend days, weeks, and months learning that he's even less of an asshole than I thought he was. That he's actually a good person, a good man. Because I'm pretty sure I could learn it. I could learn to like him. My body already does, but whatever, my body is a traitor. She just likes to participate in the O's Ash gives. And he gives super amazing O's. Yeah, my body's on board, but what's even more dangerous is that my mind and my heart could get on board too.

I have to remember that it's the curse.

The curse of Ash's dick.

Shut up. That is not helpful.

Whatever. You know it's true. Your fingers are a poor substitute, and you're not brave enough to buy sex toys, so what can I say?

Maybe my internal voice is more like an internal dialogue with my lady cave.

Whatever the curse, be it the curse of the ring, the curse of Ash's dick, the curse of finding out how exciting it is to have him participate in orgasms or whatever, or even if it's the curse of kindness, it *is* still some kind of curse, which means it's not real. How many times have I heard the old adage about feelings not being facts? As in, don't trust that shit, don't trust the afterglow, don't trust swelling heart feels, and don't trust your gut reaction. Wait, maybe you're supposed to trust that one.

Ugh, this is such a bloody mess.

I can hear Ash's heart beating beneath my ear, and it's making things wonky. His breathing is getting deep and slow, which means he's going to fall asleep. I'm still trapped in the circle of his arms, squished up against his big, sweaty chest. His heavy legs are tangled up with mine, pinning me down, and his breathing tickles my forehead. It all feels *so* good.

But I *know* it's not right.

Ash might have helped me in some pretty obvious ways and in some non-obvious ways too. He helped my dad, and it all feels really nice, but there are facts I can't forget or escape. His family still damaged ours. I can't just forget that and begin to forgive it.

Plus, my boss is still waiting for a story. I still need a job and want to keep my job. It might not be where I imagined myself working or where I wanted to end up, but it's a foot in the door into the industry I love and have always wanted to work in. This could be my big chance to get somewhere. To make enough money to pay my dad's bills and keep paying for his therapy once Ash figures out I betrayed him, starts hating my family and me, and stops doing us any more favors. I could give the story to my boss, or I could take it somewhere else, sell it, and probably not have to work very hard for a long time to come. At least I could take care of some of our worries and check off a couple of boxes on the long list of things I need to pay for but can't because my salary sucks.

That's a fact. I know I have to betray Ash. I mean, it's not like I'm really his maid. And even if I were, he would fire me after this, so yeah. No story, no job. No fake job as a maid, no paycheck. No paycheck, no apartment. No apartment means I'd have to move in with my dad, and even though that wouldn't be horrible or anything, it still wouldn't help us pay the bills or keep him going to therapy.

And what if I didn't betray Ash? What if I took this, ran with it, and we learned together that maybe love isn't such a fucked up thing, and it's possible to start somewhere and make a good go of it? My parents did, after all. They lost out in the end, but they never lost their love. My mom had to leave before any of us were ready, but we all still love her like crazy. Maybe Ash and I could have that.

No, that's just crazy. It's the curse.

Ash's heartbeat goes on steadily beneath my ear, and his warmth surrounds me. His scent is all rich and spicy and sweaty when I inhale, and yes, it's a good smell. It's the smell of twisted sheets, wild romps, and pleasure I never thought possible. It's also the smell of rightness, a good connection, and something I've never experienced with anyone.

It's the curse. The curse, I tell you, the curse.

Whomp, whomp, whomp. Ash's heartbeat goes on steadily. His breaths are deep and even, with a little snort on the end of one that is so adorable, it makes my heart want to break into a thousand tiny pieces. Already. *It can't be happening already. This man is my enemy, my way out. This man needs to be served some ice-cold vengeance.*

But he did not do anything. It was all his granny's fault.

Still. Him and me, we have no future.

My hand is nestled on Ash's solid chest, right by my face. I open my eyes and stare into the surface of the ring. It flashes back at me like a wink.

Oh my god. Oh my god, it's so obvious. All this time...

I know how to break the curse.

I might not want to, but I have to. Because. This. Isn't. Real. Life. It would never work. It's better that I just wreck everything now, and we hurt a little in our own respective ways than it is to hurt a lot later when we get attached and, of course, things don't work out.

Most of the time, these things never work out.

I carefully detach myself from Ash, which involves a good few minutes of slowly untangling our legs and getting out from under his heavy, protective, and muscly arm. I leave him lying there, in his big bed. Alone. But I do pull the sheet and blanket up around him. Because New Orleans is so cold in the summer and all that, not because I actually care.

I'm as silent and deadly as a fart—maybe not the best simile to use here, but I guess it's true—as I tiptoe down the hallway to the guest bedroom where I have my things. The door has a lock on it, which is useful when committing entirely nefarious deeds.

I pull out the laptop I brought over with my change of clothes, take out my recorder, and get to work.

16

ASH

Mornings have never been my strong point, but I've never hallucinated before—case in point, the flashy ring on my nightstand.

Wait, what? What flashy ring on my nightstand?

I come awake with a jerk, tug the blankets off, and stand myself upright. Then, I grab the ring and inspect it, thinking it must be some kind of joke. Did Ellis have a fake one made? Is this her way of getting me back for the towel incident? Although, I suppose that ended with our mutual enjoyment.

Did she spend the night in my bed? I look all around like an idiot before I realize she's not here now. Seriously, mornings aren't for me. I have to blink several times and rake my hands through my hair fiercely before my brain kicks in, and it registers that no, she's not here, and no, she didn't get a fake ring made. This isn't a joke. She got the ring off.

After we had sex.

Sex that felt intimate and right and connected. My maleness and pride know when someone is faking an orgasm. Well, it's pretty simple to deduce that Ellis wasn't faking it because why would she go to the trouble of faking it multiple times? She was for sure into it. If she weren't, she wouldn't have ridden my face and all the other stuff.

Was it too soon? Is that what broke the curse? Did I fuck everything up with my potential soulmate by falling into bed with her?

Hold up. Potential soulmate? Am I really starting to believe the curse? Wait, not starting. Do I honestly believe it? And what about the L word?

I stumble around, locate a pair of fresh boxers, and slip them on. No need to go downstairs in the nude in case Ellis is still here, having a cup of coffee. She probably wouldn't appreciate the full male frontal walking around. I know it's an art form, but I'm sure there's a time and a place for it—say in a museum, on statues made of stone, or in paintings. Not in my kitchen.

I throw on a t-shirt just for extra decency, then go with jeans too, because why not? I might as well be fully dressed when I ask a thousand questions about how she got the ring off.

I hit the stairs, my brain burning up inside my skull.

How? How did she get the ring off? How did she think to try again? Why now? I have to say my dick is totally insulted. Right, I'm not going to mention that.

The kitchen is empty. In fact, the whole house is eerily silent. I leap back up the stairs, taking them four at a time—and nope, no faceplants or dickplants—and dash down the hall to Ellis' room. The door is unlocked when I try it. The bed is neatly made, and all her things are gone.

Suddenly, a shrill buzzing explodes in my head. I nearly fall into the wall and have to grip the door so hard that if it were a lesser made door, it probably would have torn clean off the hinges. Then, I realize the sudden sound isn't my house exploding or imploding, and it's not the curse blowing up in my face. It's just my phone, ringing from my room and the pocket of the jeans I wore yesterday. I have a clear mental picture of it, and it momentarily cancels out my doom premonition.

I rush to answer it before whoever it is on the line hangs up. *It might be Ellis. Please let it be Ellis.*

Sadly, nope. It's my granny. Normally, I wouldn't heave out a sigh and dread the worst—well, maybe sometimes, because when it comes to Granny, you never know—but now, I do sigh and dread the worst, although I still answer the call and force my voice to be normal.

"The ring," Granny pants in her scratchy granny voice. "Where's the ring?"

"Uh, I have it." This is just getting creepy. I feel like I've been thrust into a B-grade horror film, and this is right where the things that sketchily climb the ceiling, the ghosts and ghouls, and the guy with a chainsaw make an appearance.

"You have it? Or Ellis has it?"

"Wait. How do you know her name? I didn't even get a chance to properly introduce you when you were here."

Granny makes a scratchy noise into the phone. It's the kind of noise that scares me senseless—worse than a ranting, raving guy with a chainsaw fired up—because she only makes that noise when something terrible happens.

"Anyway, I have it," I clarify in a very unmanly sounding squeak.

"Shit," Granny curses. "Double shit. All the shit." Then, she sighs. "You thought you could fool the curse, but in the end, it outdid you."

This is getting sketchier by the minute. "What are you talking about?"

"Your family made all their money in the newspaper and magazine industry, and you haven't even turned on the TV or checked your phone yet?"

"I generally avoid doing that first thing in the morning because I find it's often the quickest way to spoil a day."

"You're an artist," Granny grumbles. "Don't you need a good dose of heavy sadness to inspire you?"

"Ugh, Granny, listen, I—"

"No, you listen here. Whatever you did, you need to fix it. The ring wouldn't come off Ellis' finger for a reason, and now you have it, which means she broke the curse. It doesn't mean she's not your soulmate, but it means she's found a way around it."

"I...how do you know this?" The dots align as soon as I ask that dumb question. Granny knows Ellis' name, and she asked me if I'd seen the news or turned on my phone, which means there's something on there. A story of some sort. About. Me?

"There's a story about you," Granny snaps, confirming my worst suspicions. "Broke this morning. She sold it to a publication in LA. An online sleazy thing. They broke it, and now my phone won't stop ringing. Everyone wants to know if it's true that my grandson and Meryl Burbank were planning on entering into a fake marriage. More than that, people want to know about the cursed ring. I've had buyers offering me ten times the price for it. Ten times, damn it."

Holy fuckshit, what? Ellis wrote a story about Meryl and me? She sold it to someone, and they published it? And now everyone wants to get their hands on the ring? She must have known the cursed ring is worth a lot, more so now, but she didn't take it. Why?

Duh. Probably because it has a fuck ton of bad voodoo attached to it, and she no longer wanted to be cursed.

Perhaps she thought selling it would curse her for the rest of her life, and she didn't want to take a chance on it.

She appears to have washed her hands off me. And not only did she get the ring off, but I think she was lying to me the whole time.

"She was lying to you the whole time," Granny barks.

Good god, it's creepy how she can read my thoughts like that.

"How do you know that?"

"It was in the story too. About how she pretended to be your maid and went undercover. I suppose you did hire her, but she was looking for an in. I thought she looked familiar when I saw her, but I couldn't place her. Now I know. She's the daughter of Bob Hunter. He owned a small newspaper here. I bought it out and shut it down since it wasn't profitable. I did promise him I'd keep it running, and that was my intention when I bought it, but it just didn't make sense after running the numbers. There were people who lost their jobs because of it, including him, I'm sorry to say."

Oh my god, Ellis' dad. "I did something kind for her dad," I blurt. Now I'm committed, and I can't stop. Granny won't let me get away with it. She'll pester me to death by asking questions. "I...she told me before she introduced us that I couldn't use my name. She asked me to just say I was a friend. When I asked her the reason, she said it was because her dad thought I was an asshole. She always thought I was an asshole. She made no secret about that."

"So, your soulmate actually came to you hating you because she wanted revenge for something our family did to hers."

"Her dad was really depressed, and it was bad. I thought it was because her mom died. She did say it was years ago, but some people never get over it. So I wanted to help. I know a good therapist; one mom went to see, and I managed to convince him to give it a try. She was so relieved. She was...she...it meant everything to her. And she was willing to let me help. I guess, in a weird way, I was fixing our family's mistakes even though I didn't know it."

"But she still sold you out."

"No, I...she..." Did she sell me out? That sounds cheap and so very not like Ellis. But what do I really know about her? Nothing. I'm surprised Ellis is even her real name.

"I had some guys look into her background this morning after I read the story. She's a journalist who works for a crappy online publication. Or I should say, she did. Apparently, she sent in her notice late last night. I'm assuming right before or after she sent the article off to someone else.

"Granny, she probably needed the money. She lives in a crappy apartment building, and her dad isn't doing well. He's not working, and his house is tiny and old. I don't know how he's paying his bills. She's probably paying them."

"Hmm," Granny grunts. "So you're defending her. Interesting."

Why the deuce *am* I defending her? "I mean, we did wreck something very dear to her family, and it sent her dad into a tailspin. She probably thought she had every right. But it doesn't explain why the ring wouldn't come off her finger, though. If she was going to betray me the whole time."

"It probably came off after she did it. She likely thought that betraying you would break the curse. Before, she hadn't done it. She was just thinking about it. She could have changed her mind."

"It...it felt like she might. Things felt...different. She wasn't accusing me of being an asshole anymore, and it was almost like...I felt it. I felt that, as corny and ridiculous as it is to say it, we had a connection. We felt right together."

"Mmm. So you bumped uglies with her."

"Granny! That is none of your business!"

"Ha! My guess is she felt you were getting too close. That maybe things were a little bit too right. She knew all about your plan to fake a marriage so you would never have to risk falling in love, and she knew all about you not believing in curses or love. She wrote it in her article, so don't ask me how I know. I can't believe you, your brother, and your cousins made a pact to thwart the curse. Let me tell you, sonny, it ain't gonna work." Great. Granny only talks slang when she's really pissed. Or thoroughly disgusted. I suppose she could probably be that too. "The curse is meant to help you. It's meant to get through your thick head and thick skin, and it's meant to make you happy! I watched my sons give up their families and shred their lives apart. I watched how it hurt your mother and aunt and how it hurt you kids. I had to go through every single painful step knowing it was my fault for making those boys who they were."

"Granny, it wasn't your fault. Sometimes people do shitty things, and sometimes they just do wrong, no matter how right you raise them."

Granny's voice becomes softer, and so does her sigh. "Thank you, Asherly." She's the only one who still calls me that, and usually, it rankles me, but not today. Today, it feels like an endearment. "Thank you for saying so. I'm glad you don't blame me for what happened."

"Blame you?" I can't believe she just said that. "No, I don't blame you!"

"Good. Good. I'm glad. But I'm not glad that you thought you could fake a marriage in order to save yourself from the very thing that could set you free, though."

I go to sit down hard on the edge of the bed and end up sliding down like the damn thing is a metal slide greased up with butter at the playground. I hit the floor hard enough to bite my tongue clean in half.

"What was that?" Granny asks.

"What was what?" I groan.

"What was that bang?"

"Nothing."

"You sure it wasn't karma?"

I roll my eyes and stick out my tongue to make sure I just bit it and that no lasting damage has been done. It's still there in one piece, so I guess I'll live, even if my mouth tastes like I just sucked on the back end of a copper pipe.

"What about Meryl in all of this?" Granny continues.

"Christ. Meryl. She's going to be mortified."

"Lucky for you, that's a trick question. Ellis didn't name the woman, but from the way she was described, I knew who she was. Most people won't since you never made your engagement public. You were seen together a few times, but you're both private people, which is a good thing. People might figure it out, though, so she might want to lay low for a couple of weeks, but it will blow over. I'm more hurt than you are in all this. I can't believe you were going to lie to me like that. Your own granny, who loves and cherishes you beyond anything else in the world."

"What about your other grandkids?"

"I meant all of you and your mother and aunt too. Even my sons, for all the mistakes they made and the harm they've done. I love all of you. You're my family. You never had to lie to me and try and fake your way out of the curse because it was going to get you sooner or later. The question is, what are you going to do to get your soulmate back?"

I nearly drop the phone. "Excuse me? I don't think she wants to come back."

"You know what I think? I think you should pop your

noggin out of the dark hole that serves as your rumpus and get your ducks in a dang line."

"Granny, no one has a dark hole for a rump. The dark hole would be part of the rump."

Granny cackles. "You must be feeling better if you're making jokes. So here's what you're going to do. You're going to find the girl and tell her it's okay she sold you out even though it's not, but that you understand why she did it, and you forgive her. It will prove to her that you're not a heartless asshole. You can blame it on me if you like, but it wasn't you who did anything wrong. She probably already knows that, so I'm guessing it wasn't about revenge for her anymore. She did it because she was scared. It's a lot to put on a stranger—soulmate stuff, a curse, a ring. Way too much for her to handle in just a few days. Then you added something else to it, or maybe she did, though I personally think you both did. You added your feelings into the mix. Your heart, boy, the one thing you promised to always leave out. You come off like you're busy trying to build walls to protect yourself, but really, you just want to let someone in. You're aching to do it, but it's hard. And she ran because she's scared. She thinks you don't believe in love and don't want it. The ring was a symbol of everything you didn't want, and you wanted it off her hand. That was your common goal. Hardly a good start. No wonder she was frantic."

"So you want me to what? Bring the ring back and force it onto her?"

"Are you seriously that dense, Ash, because I swear—"

"You want me to find her and tell her how I feel. How I started to feel, at any rate. You want me to put it out there that I'd like to get to know her minus the curse. That I'd like to take my time getting to know her, and one day, maybe she'll be my soulmate and get the ring anyway, and that maybe I'd want her to have it."

Granny hoots a cackly laugh straight into my ear. "Dear lord, boy, I hope you come up with something better than that. Finesse. It's all about finesse. Use the right words. Not flowery shit but good shit. Anyway, just find her before it's too late."

"What about the article?"

"Leave that to me. I'm not a force to be reckoned with for nothing. People know they can't fuck with my family. I'll squash the article and make sure it's removed from every outlet that published it. Don't worry about how much it's going to cost. I'll take care of the details. You just go and get your soulmate back."

"What if she doesn't want to have anything to do with me?"

"Tough luck. The ring chose her, and she's cursed. It's better to be cursed with you than cursed apart. Maybe try that line. It's quite lyrical."

Click.

My granny just hung up. I slowly shake my head and set the phone down. Sadly, my mouth still tastes like copper and bitter regret. How did I not see this coming? Why did I act the way I did? I have to phone Meryl and apologize for this, and I have to do all this damage control now. I hurt people and humiliated others, but I did all that because I was running away scared like a buffoon.

However, Granny was right about one thing. In trying to avoid love or at least something that feels pretty nice and warm and funny in my chest—or attachment because let's go with safer words for now—I ran straight into it. Why that's no longer a horrifying prospect, I'm not entirely sure. I just know the old terror that used to strike sure and deep every time I thought about the concept isn't there anymore.

Instead, Ellis' face is. She's there, laughing, smiling, and joyful. She's there with the frustration and sorrow brimming in her eyes when she left her dad's house the first night, and she's there with the relief, gratitude, and love when he wrapped his arms around her the second night. She's there soaking her hand in oil to try and get the ring off, she's there with a look of wonder at getting our tarot cards reading, and she's there covered in paint after attempting an abstract art herself. She's there, dripping wet from the shower and in the black dress my cousin brought for her, she's there in her loose jeans and her long-sleeved shirt, she's there in her blouse soaked with dishwater, and she's there with her eyes closed and lips parted while in the throes of pleasure.

She's there, and that's the point. She's so firmly there that there is no digging her out. There is no running in the opposite direction, and this is just after a few days. I can't imagine what it would be like after a few weeks, a month, years, a lifetime. I should want to run and give the ring to some unsuspecting soul before getting the heck out of New Orleans for good. I should also want to hire another fake fiancé or get another fake wife to save me from making the mistakes of my father, doing harm, and having it all go to shit.

But maybe mistakes don't always have to be bad. I already know I'd never do what my father did. I'd never hurt another person that way. Yes, things don't always work out, but sometimes it can be amicable. People do grow apart, but they don't always have to. They can respect one another, and they can actually try. If the divorce rate is fifty percent, as I always liked to point out, then it's technically a glass half full, half-empty kind of scenario. It means just as many people make it as those who don't.

And it means I'm a glass half full kind of hopeful if you ask me.

I would never have admitted it before. I'm the son of a man who left his wife in the messiest, meanest way possible, who abandoned his family, and who didn't care whether he heard from his children or not for months or even years at a time. I'm the child of a broken marriage, but I'm also the son of a mother who didn't abandon her children. A mother who fought like hell to get over what happened to her and give us a good childhood. I'm the child of a man who eventually wanted to mend his ways and bridge the gap back into my life. And I'm the child of a family held together by our love for each other, even through adversity. I include my brother, cousins, and aunt in this because we all came together. And, of course, my granny. I always saw love through the eyes of my dad leaving us, but I was looking at it wrong. That wasn't what love is. Love is what my mom and aunt did for us, and love is how they stayed. Love is my brother and cousins, and love is my crazy meddling Granny cursing us all because she couldn't bear for us not to have it.

Good god, I've been an epic shit-linger.

I scramble off the floor and grab my phone. I have to think fast. I have calls to make, apologies galore to give, a painting to wrap up, delivery to schedule, and a noggin to pull out of my rumpus. Oh, and a potential soulmate to try and get back. That's quite a lot for a single morning, so I best get started.

17

ELLIS

You know the nasty feeling of anxiety you get where you've done something extraordinarily terrible, and you're pretty sure you're either going to get sued or arrested unless you act fast and freaking up and get your ass to Switzerland with a fake ID, a wig, and maybe some plastic surgery to change your face? Um, yeah. That's me right now.

Pacing my apartment.

And no, I don't have a bugout bag packed.

Before I wrote the article, I sent a couple of feeler emails to some shitty magazines. It wasn't hard to get their contact info. When working in the industry, it's easy to find it. I got a response back immediately even though it was well in the middle of the night. Yes, they wanted the story, and yes, they were willing to pay for it. After I wrote the article at Ash's house, in the guest room, and sent it off, I tested the ring, and it slid off my finger like it was three sizes too big. I held it in my right hand for a while as tears streamed down my face. I was a mess of snot and red eyes before I could even think about gathering my few things together and getting out of there.

Ash slept through it all. He slept through me ruining his life, setting the ring on his nightstand while I tried so hard not to look at his exquisitely beautiful—in a rugged manly way—face, and me making a fast getaway and going back to my apartment. I can only imagine how he woke up this morning.

I've been imagining it ever since I got to my apartment and crammed myself onto the window ledge in my living room just because it overlooks the street. While I tried to figure out what my next move would be, I chewed my fingernails down to nothing, and then I checked my bank account and was shocked to see that a ten thousand dollar payment had gone in. It was the amount I agreed on. I knew selling the story wouldn't make me a millionaire or anything. But this is enough money to take care of a good portion of my student loans, pay most of my dad's outstanding bills, and get me through at least the next month while I find another job, though I might never work in New Orleans again. I realize I might have shot myself in the foot by publishing the story. Ash's granny might see to it that no one will ever hire me.

Regardless, I tell myself it isn't the worst thing in the world. The job wasn't what I thought it would be anyway. I really only wanted to be a journalist so I could work with my dad and make him proud, but I can now scratch the latter off my list because I'm never going to make him proud with what I did. I know he'll find out because I used my real name when the story was published. I didn't want to take the coward's way out. It's not going to make him any sort of proud even if he finds out I did it for him. Instead, he'll probably be mad at me for a good long while, and things will be strained. Maybe when I promise him I'll never do anything like it again—mostly because I think I'm giving up on being a journalist—then he'll find it in his heart to forgive me.

After sitting by the window and watching the street for the remaining part of the night, I forced myself to drag a slightly more comfortable kitchen chair over, sit my bottom down, and make a list of all the jobs I can get with my current degree. There are quite a few actually since I know companies would hire me for their communications department. At least, I hope.

Maybe I'll have to move away from here before I can get another job. I guess I should have thought of that before I acted like a big sleaze head. I'd like to tell myself I wouldn't have done it if it weren't for the curse, and I'd like to believe it too. Except it makes me seem soft-hearted, and when it comes to the Cromwells, I never want to be that.

Do I feel regret?

Yes. Yes, I do. Ash wasn't an asshole after all. He turned out to be a really nice guy, and hey, even if his art isn't my flavor, whatever. Some people like it, so good on him. He might be spoiled and have advantages I don't have, but he was quick to help someone who needed it—my dad—even though the someone was a complete stranger. Ash didn't harm my family personally. He was just the one person I could get at in order to stick pins into the Cromwells. I wanted to give up on my plan after I got to know Ash. I swear I did. It was the curse, though. I couldn't just walk around with the ring stuck to my hand, believing I was his soulmate for what...the rest of my life? That would have been crazy.

This was the only way I could think to do it and save us both a lot of trouble ahead. It truly sucks right now, but it's for the best. If I could have thought of any other way to get the ring off, I would have done it. Well, short of cutting my finger off because I wouldn't have done that. No matter how many times it was suggested, the idea never grew on me.

It's morning now, and I feel like a wreck. By now, Ash has to know what happened. No one has shown up at my door yet, buzzing my apartment and demanding for me to come down. No one from the media, no lawyers come to serve my ass with a lawsuit, no angry granny, no vengeful brother or cousins, and no ex-soulmate.

I need to get my act together. I need to get off this chair, which I've been perched on for the past few hours, even though it's pretty much as uncomfortable as the window ledge. I need to shower, change my clothes, brush my teeth, and start on damage control.

I better start working on my resume too.

God, I am so fucked.

I'm just scraping my rather numb behind off the chair and stretching my arms above my head to work out the kinks when a very familiar black sedan pulls up at the curb in front of the building.

"Shit!" I immediately drop down and belly crawl to the window so I can't be seen. "Holy shit. Crap. Fuck. Shit fuck. Crap shit fuck." I drag myself up to peep above the ledge, and yup. It's Granny, alright. Sans ballgown and in a more regular pink pantsuit—did I just call a pantsuit regular??—she's still pretty gorgeous. And Ash is right beside her. Also, I note that in a regular t-shirt and jeans, he's as gorgeous as ever.

"Fuck," I hiss again. I scramble away from the window and...and what?

Where exactly am I supposed to go? I could throw together a bag real fast, grab my laptop, my phone, and my keys before bailing out the back door, getting in my car, and heading to my dad's, but they'd probably try there next. I can't just abandon Dad. If I have to leave New Orleans, it's going to break his heart. It'll break mine too, knowing I did all this to try and avenge him, when really, all I did was play with guns and shoot us both in the foot with bullets.

"Fudge my life with the fudgiest fudge."

The buzzer rings. I let out a screech, rush to the kitchen, and grab a frying pan. If they've come to fuck me up, then I'll be ready. Goddamn it, I knew Granny had underworld connections when I saw her car.

Oh really? Where are her goons then? Because Ash and his granny are walking up to the door alone. The goons are probably around back, kicking in the back door to make sure I can't escape. Or maybe they're coming. Ash and his granny are walking up all innocent and sweet, but the goons will probably follow once they're in place.

Who am I kidding? Ash's granny is badass enough that she wouldn't need goons to dispense me. She's probably packing heat in the designer handbag I saw looped around her small arm.

The buzzer goes off again. Should I answer? Is it worse to try and avoid my fate, or should I just face it? Maybe they've come with bribe money. It could be that they want to pay me for damage control, to say I made the whole thing up. Perhaps I should just get whatever this is out of the way so we can all move on. I put my name on the article for a reason. Because I didn't want to be a coward. So why am I hiding up here now?

I make a quick decision. If I go to the front door, they probably can't murder me there or fuck me up or whatever because people would see. It's like somewhere around ten or eleven in the morning, so there have to be people outside walking and driving by—witnesses.

I head out of my apartment and down the two flights of stairs to the front door. I don't even realize I'm still clutching the frying pan until I open the glass front door, and Ash stares right at it before he even looks at me.

"What are you doing with that?" his granny asks. She sounds pleasant and not at all like she's got a secret handgun she's about to use on me. Or maybe a set of brass knuckles. I could see her donning those. They'd suit her well.

I bring the frying pan up and look at it before swiftly tucking it behind my back with both hands. "Uh, I was cooking eggs," I mumble. "Yeah. Eggs."

"But they weren't in the pan?" Granny's brows shoot up.

"No. I, uh, was just about to crack them when the buzzer rang."

"Oh, good. Breakfast. I'm starved. We could all head up and—"

"No! I...that's alright. Whatever you have to say, just do it right here." I clench my eyes shut for a second while I fist the frying pan's handle so hard that it will probably be embedded in both my hands for life. *She's trying to lure me upstairs to finish me off. She's not even trying to be subtle about it.*

When I open my eyes, Granny doesn't look mad. She's actually looking at Ash, who is now this sludgy gray color. He still manages to look handsome, though, but I guess that's the kind of color for someone who just got his life half destroyed by a tabloid article written by his ex-cursed-ex-soulmate.

"Go on," Granny urges, and I brace myself. Is she ordering him to fuck me up because she doesn't want to get her hands dirty? "I wanted to come with him because I didn't trust him not to mess this up."

That does it. I brace myself like a ninja, legs spread apart and one hand gripping the frying pan above my head, ready to strike. "Come one step closer, and I swear I'll scream. I'll also knock you senseless with this frying pan if you lay a finger on me. No one will believe it wasn't self-defense. You found out about the article, came here in a murderous rage to try and break my kneecaps, and I knocked you a good one. I'll have the whole jury on my side."

Ash's brows rocket up to match his granny's. Beside him, his granny slaps her thighs, bends over double, and lets out a wild burst of laughter that people can probably hear five miles away. I'm shocked the glass doesn't blast out of the front door since it's so loud.

"Oh god. Child, we're not here to hurt you. Dear sweet Jesus, what were you thinking? If I wanted to do that, I would have brought thugs."

"I knew it," I mutter.

I glance at the car by the curb. The big burly driver is sitting in the front seat.

"Oh, him? That's my driver," Granny chuckles. "I'm tupping him. That's why he came."

"I knew it," Ash mutters.

"No, we're not here because we want to do something to you or cause trouble for you. We're here because we wanted to tell you that we understand why you did what you did. I now know why you wanted to write the story in the first place. I'm sorry I had to shut your father's paper down after I bought it. The truth is, I promised I wouldn't, but it just wasn't making any money. I know a lot of people lost their jobs, but I do want you to know I offered each and every one of them a position in my other companies. Some took the jobs, but some refused, like your father. I did try to make things right. I'm sorry your dad wasn't well after it happened. I didn't mean to hurt anyone. I thought I was just doing business as usual. I did pay a fair price for his paper, but I know you probably saw it as a personal loss, and so did your dad. I didn't know you were struggling with other losses, or I would have checked in. I would have personally come and explained why I had to do what I did."

I have to scrape my mouth up from around the level of my knees. I can't believe what I'm hearing. "I...yes, ma'am. I'm sorry that I...that I did what I did."

"Did you do it because you hated my family and me, or did you do it to break the curse?" Ash asks. He's remarkably self-composed, and his face now has a little more color in it, too, I'm relieved to see.

I turn and set the frying pan down on the stairs. I guess I won't be needing it for beatings or to stave off beatings. "I... because...well, I couldn't just keep the ring on my finger forever. What were we going to do? Just leave it there and hope the curse works itself out? Or were you getting serious about cutting my finger off?"

"You threatened to cut her finger off?" Ash's granny smacks his arm.

"No! I mean, I wasn't serious!" Ash grumbles. He turns back to me while rubbing his bicep. "I wasn't serious about that, but you probably thought I wasn't serious about anything else either. That I wasn't into the soulmates thing and the curse, or even love. You heard all of it, the pact my cousins, my brother, and I made. You knew I've been running from it my whole life and that I was even willing to invent a fake marriage to get away from it."

"Yeah, I did."

"I don't blame you for being scared or for thinking I'd bail on you the first chance I got."

"But I…I thought you wanted the ring off as badly as I did. I knew it wasn't going to work out. Ever. The stuff we felt was just because of the curse. Even if it were real, what kind of future would that be for us? None. It was a mistake, both the ring and the curse. It was never supposed to be me."

"I'm not so sure about that." Ash looks at me with this raw sparkle in his eye and an even rawer expression. He's looking at me with an epic amount of vulnerability here, and he's leaving himself fully open.

"What?" I gasp. "What are you talking about?"

"He's talking about having a change of heart," Granny pipes up. She's got a huge grin on her face again, so big that her dentures are threatening to pop out like the first time I saw her smile at me. "He's talking about opening his mind and heart and realizing he's got a lot to figure out yet. That he doesn't want to live his life without love. He told me his glass was always half-empty, but now he wants it to be half full. I told him that was token and idiotic, and I better come along to stop him from making a big fool out of himself, botching this, and losing you all over again. Because he doesn't want to do that. He wants to get to know you. He wants to take you on proper dates, woo you, wine and dine you, and make you realize just how special you are. And then he'd like to tup you again, I'm sure."

"Grannnnnnnnnnyyyyyyyy!"

I can't take it. I burst out laughing. I throw my head back and let the peals of laughter roll through me. My god, at the very least, this is wildly entertaining. Too bad I didn't make popcorn.

"Is she telling the truth?" I ask when I can get something out between my laughter.

"Damn tootin' I am," Granny insists.

Ash nods. "Yeah." He gives his grandmother a foul look that I can tell he doesn't mean, and then he looks back at me, and his face is all open and soft again, still gorgeous—man-gorgeous. "Yes, she's telling the truth. I *do* want to get to know you, and I want to prove I'm not an asshole. I felt something with you that I've never felt in my entire life. I honestly didn't even believe in it. Not the curse but love. Not that I'm saying I'm in love. That's crazy, and it would be frightening and too fast, but I did feel connected to you. I felt...I had so much fun with you, trying to get the stupid ring off and also trying to beat the curse. Although, to be honest, I didn't feel one bit cursed at all. I actually felt blessed. You shared your life with me. All your secrets and those bits you were scared to let everyone else see, like your dad. You even told me about your mom. You opened yourself up, and I know you probably don't do that, but it didn't seem that hard for you to do it with me, and I could just see you. The kind, amazing, wild, smart, and beautiful Ellis."

"I think you mean conniving, double-crossing, back-stabbing, betraying—"

"No, I don't mean that. I don't mean that at all."

"And it's not just because he wants to tup you," Granny supplies helpfully.

Ash's left eye twitches violently. "No, it's not just because of that. I had fun, Ellis. I felt like we...I don't know. I've never felt what I felt before, and it was nice. I realized what an idiot I was being and how wrong I'd looked at everything. My brother and cousins are going to see me as a traitor to our pact, but it's okay because they're all cursed too, and I now believe it's real, so eventually, they will all fall in love too, and then they'll realize why I had to do it."

"Whoa," I breathe. "Just...whoa..."

"I also wanted you to know that I'd like to make things right with your dad. Even if you never want to see me again or spend another minute trying to figure out if maybe the curse was onto something, even if you wouldn't like to let me take you out or get to know me or even stick me in the friendzone, I wanted him to have one of my paintings. It's the first painting I ever exhibited. It's worth somewhere around twenty million, but I've never agreed to sell it because it was my first one. You know, the first is always special."

Granny titters at that. "Ha! I can't even remember my first. And don't think it was your grandfather. People weren't saints back then; the world just thinks they were."

Ash and I both blush at the same time, though Granny does not blush. In fact, she is clearly proud of herself for that bit of information. My god, it would be wonderful to be related to this woman, even if I used to think the exact opposite.

"Anyway..." Ash clears his throat. "I want your dad to have it. He can sell it if he wants. There are quite a few people who would like to get their hands on it, so if he sells it at an auction, he could probably even get more for it. I don't want you to think I'm trying to buy you back or bribe you by offering to take care of your dad if you're with me. That's the last thing I want. I want you to just be you while you're getting to know who I truly am. I think it could work. If you're up for it."

I search his face for signs of anger, tricks, or something asshole-ish or less than good, but there is nothing at all but *goodness and kindness*. Then, I search myself for the urge to escape, the rising tide of panic that happens when I feel trapped, and the gut feeling I've always listened to. I even search myself for inner angst and all that sort of stuff, but I come up with nothing. Nothing negative, at least. Because all I feel is *goodness and kindness.*

"So you're not mad about the article?" At this point, I'm starting to think I'm hallucinating, so I had better double-check.

"No, I'm not mad."

"But Meryl—"

"She'll be okay. In a weird way, the article did her a favor. Her dad is of the mindset that no publicity is bad publicity, and he's already agreed to lay off her about getting married now that he knows she was going to consider a fake marriage just so she could please him and get some peace."

"So she's not mad? And you're not mad?" It's almost too much to believe and hope for. That all this might turn out okay. I know I have no right to ask for it to be okay, and I have no right to forgiveness. I did what I did, and no matter why I did it, I have to own it. Still, I keep holding my breath, hoping that maybe, just maybe, all the things I never knew I wanted might come true.

Ash slowly shakes his head, and my heart leaps. "No one is mad. At least she's not, and I'm not. I was shocked, and a little bit hurt. But then I—"

"He pulled his noggin out of his rumpus, got his act together, and figured out why you did it. Then, I talked more sense into him, and he realized he didn't want to live without you, so he's here."

"Yeah," Ash mutters with a shrug. He's clearly given up trying to refute his granny or make her behave. "Yeah, that's why I'm here. That's a good way of putting it, actually. I realized I didn't want to repeat my parent's mistakes. I didn't want to end up hurt and lonely, so I made myself lonely on purpose. I guess it doesn't make a lot of sense when I put it that way, but it's what I was doing. Anyway, Granny's right. I don't want to live without you in my life. I was hoping we could move slowly at first, then we can build up to something wonderful, or at least that's how I see it working out in my head."

"Slowly?" Granny snorts. "Why does everyone say slowly? I married your grandpa after a week."

"I never knew that!" Ash blusters. "What? Are you for real?"

Granny winks at me. "That's a story for another time. Or maybe right now if you'd like to join us for coffee."

Dang, she's smooth, and she's a very, very clever woman. No, it wouldn't be so bad to have her in my life. It wouldn't be so bad at all, even if she's an Asswell. I mean a Cromwell.

"Yeah." I shrug. "Okay. I...yeah...but I have a better idea. I seriously need a shower. Do you want to come up for eggs? We can have coffee up there too," I say before I look at the car. "And your driver?"

Granny winks. "I'm not really tupping him. I just said that to annoy Ash...or am I?"

"Either way, does he want eggs?"

"Noooo," Granny says. "He doesn't eat. He's actually a robot."

Ash's right eye twitches violently this time as I throw my head back and laugh. "Okay, eggs, coffee, and a good romantic story. I'm all in."

"Good," Granny says. "After I tell mine, you can both tell me yours. You never did fill me in the other night, and I had to read about it in the tabloids. Not much in there is ever true, so maybe you'll tell me the real story."

Ash grins at me, and I smile shyly back. I feel funny

inside, all bubbly and light like champagne. Is this hope? Is this what falling for someone feels like? I always thought it would hurt a lot, like faceplanting onto cement, but this is quite okay.

"Invite the robot," I prod Ash. "It's the right thing to do."

"I like her already!" Granny grins.

I can totally tell that not only is her driver not a robot, but she *really* is *tupping* him for reals.

EPILOGUE

ASH

Who can say their love story started with a curse? I'm sure people would say they were cursed right from the start, but that's not what I mean. I mean a real curse. Because I can, and I know a few others who can too. Well, maybe not yet, but they will on short order, I'm sure. My cousins, my brother, and their cursed heirlooms, I mean. I won't be the only Cromwell with one heck of a wild, absurd, and incredible love story.

My house is buzzing with family and friends, all here to wish us the best as we step into this next phase of our life. Ha. They're here for our engagement party, but it's not a step. It's not a conscious leap into something we don't know about, or hope will work out. We're not crossing our fingers. That's not why we're getting married, and it's not why Ellis agreed to put the cursed ring on for a second time. I asked her to marry me because I love her, and I am beyond sure this is not a phase but what I want for the rest of my life. And she agreed because she feels the same.

When I proposed, Ellis was more than a little hesitant

about slipping the ring back on her finger, but this time, even though it's still a good fit, it comes on and off with no issue at all, probably because both of us accepted a long time ago that we're soulmates. Or rather, not so long ago. Six months probably isn't long enough for most people, but for us, who have known from practically about day one that we were meant for each other. There isn't any right or wrong time, just the span of days where we both agree on the same thing wholeheartedly.

"I heard there was cake," Granny says, sidling up to me. "Engagement parties always have cake, don't they? Where's this promised specimen of sugary goodness?"

"In the kitchen. On the island. But please don't dip your fingers into it before we serve it."

"What about my tongue?"

"No."

"Too late," Kirian says as he sidles up beside Granny. "It's already been dipped." He holds out his finger and grins at me guiltily. "You're my big bro. I had to do something to aggravate you."

"There had better not be a fingermark in the cake." I use my best big brother threatening tone, but Kirian just laughs.

Granny punches me in the arm, and man, can she still make a fist. "Ouch!" I complain as I rub the spot.

"If I don't get to it before they do, your cousins will all take turns sampling. They never could control themselves around cakes. What flavor is the icing?"

"Tasted like all icing to me," Kirian says and shrugs.

"You better be kidding about that."

I march into the kitchen, and not only do I see that Kirian wasn't kidding because there is a giant fingermark on the edge of the cake and a hunk of icing missing, but my cousins are also sampling as I stand there.

Toren and Taylen each swipe their finger along the edge and put the gooey white icing into their mouths.

"Buttercream?" Kirian asks.

"I think so," Toren responds, licking his finger clean.

"Yeah, definitely not cream cheese. Must not be carrot cake under there," Taylen grunts, disappointed with the outcome.

"Carrot? Who likes carrot?" Toren scoffs. "You're wickedly gross."

"You're wickedly douchebag, but I don't hear me calling you out on your horrible taste," Taylen mutters. "What's wrong with carrot cake?"

"Who orders carrot cake for an engagement?" Granny asks, coming up behind me.

I shake my head. "I should have known better. I should have thwarted you all and not gotten a cake, but Ellis insisted we had to have one when I told her how much you all liked it. I also told her it would be ruined before it even got served, and she was okay with that."

"Of course she is." Leandra enters the kitchen and gives her brothers and Kirian hard looks. "Geez. You think you could behave for a few hours, but no. You have to act like little kids all the time." She shakes her head at them, but she has a smile for me. "Ellis is okay with her cake being destroyed at her engagement party because Ellis is easy-going and awesome."

"That's pretty high praise." Ellis enters the kitchen, an empty tray in her hands. She insisted on doing all the serving, catering, and getting everyone drinks even though this is supposed to be her party. She sees it more like a gathering of friends and family or a good old-fashioned barbeque since she wasn't even sure what an engagement party was supposed to be.

"You deserve it." Leandra rushes over and takes the tray from Ellis' hands. "You shouldn't be doing that. It's your party!"

"I tried to tell her, but she won't listen."

Ellis flushes with pleasure, comes to stand beside me, and loops her arm around my waist. I do the same, tucking her in tight against me. "I might be serving snacks and making sure no one goes thirsty, but this is supposed to be for everyone."

"Yeah, to celebrate you guys!" Leandra says. "And my evil brothers are eating your cake before it's time."

"That's okay. I don't mind," Ellis assures her with a wink. "We actually have a second one hidden in the fridge. It's carrot because I heard that was someone's favorite."

"Carrot?" Taylen perks up. "Fridge?"

"No way! That one you have to wait for!" Ellis exclaims.

Toren rolls his eyes. "Gross. And you two are gross too. So grossly in love. I have to admit, though, that wearing the cursed ring looks good on you, Ellis. You both actually seem happy."

"I think that's a compliment."

"Oh, it's a compliment." Leandra shakes her head at her brothers, one after the other. "It's definitely a compliment. We can't wait for Ellis to officially be a Cromwell. And we're happy the curse worked out for you, even if you did flake out of our pact."

Granny, who has been suspiciously quiet all this time, snorts. "Pact? Good god, that pact. I still can't believe you all united against me to try and thwart me. Mark my words that they'll come for you. You'll all find your soulmates and end up like Ash and Ellis. Happy and in love. Is that so bad? Is that such a terrible thing for a loving grandmother to hope for?"

"A meddling grandmother, you mean," Kirian mutters under his breath.

He narrowly avoids getting a cuff on the back of the head from Granny, who stalks quickly around the kitchen, hunting down my brother and cousins. They laugh and scatter like they're five-year-old kids getting chased out of the kitchen so they don't spoil their dinner with the tempting dessert that's laid out.

Granny just shakes her head, leaving Ellis alone with me in the kitchen.

"I know for a fact that you used to think of me as Ash Asswell. I hope you won't think of yourself as Ellis Asswell, though it does have a nice ring to it."

She twirls the cursed ring around her finger and giggles. "This ring has a nice ring to it. Even if your last name were Asswell, I'd bear it proudly." Her eyes sparkle when she looks up at me. "Thank you for all of this. I think there should be a word we use instead of the word curse because this ring was just the beginning of a ton of blessings for me."

"Oh really?" I set my hands at her waist, and she looks up at me adoringly.

"Well, we now have plants and a cat. My dad works for your granny and is happier than I've ever seen him, and I also work for your granny, which is amazing because you know how much I love my job. I've even come around to liking your art, but don't tell anyone I said that."

I laugh and bend my head to nuzzle the spot near her ear. "Don't worry. Your secret's safe with me."

She tilts her head and leans into the kiss I place on her neck. Ellis inhales sharply and pulls back just a little. I can tell by the way her eyes are shining that she's going to tell me something profound and wonderful. She does it from time to time—okay, all the time—and it's probably what I love most about her. She doesn't hold back. Not with the bad, not with the good. She's very open, and she's taught me so much about communication. She's taught me about friendship, loyalty, what it takes to make it work with someone, and how to blend two lives into one.

"You know, I feel so loved that it sometimes takes my breath away."

Only Ellis would say things like that. In my world, at least, she's the only one. I kiss her soundly before wrapping my hands around her waist and lifting her onto the island, only inches away from the cake.

"Whoa," she protests happily. "Don't ruin it for everyone. A few licks are one thing. Putting the imprint of my butt in it is another."

"Don't give me ideas."

One brow cocks deviously. "Don't or do?"

"Definitely do, but we should save them for later."

"I'll be sure to start a naughty ideas list."

"Excellent." I kiss her again, so long and hard that we're both panting after. "You steal my breath too. Literally and figuratively," I tell her. "I love you, Ellis, my cursed soulmate."

"Cursed or blessed?"

That's a very good question, and I'm glad she put it that way. I'm going to have to petition Granny to change the name of whatever she did, but I think, at this point, my brother and cousins would still call their objects cursed.

"Blessed," I say with total conviction and the biggest, dopiest smile. "Definitely blessed."

If you loved this book, then don't forget to check out the next forever cursed story, Ex for You which is Toren and Luna's story.

EX FOR YOU

LUNA

It all started with a meddling granny and a bracelet I didn't know was cursed until it was too late.

It had been mailed to me, ostensibly for cleaning. I thought it was because I ran a jewelry shop, where I made my own custom pieces and specialized in antiques. The bracelet was at least a century old, so it made perfect sense when I opened up the package and saw it, along with a note.

Dear amazing jeweler,

I'm very dirty. Cursed to be dirty, or maybe just plain cursed and dirty. Please clean me. My rightful owner will come and pick me up on Friday, at noon. Please have me ready, sparkly clean, and wonderfully pristine.

Yours truly,

The very dirty wrist grabber

Yeah, okay, it was a weird note, but this is New Orleans, and it's not the first strange thing I've received in the mail. Obviously, whoever sent it had a dry as dust sense of humor and was just trying to make things fun. I could do with a little more fun. Everyone could. There was a hundred-dollar bill tucked in with the note, so I knew the sender was serious. I know, I know. Who sends cash in the mail?

The envelope might not have had a return address, but it did have a tracking number, so whoever sent it was sure to know it was sent to the right place and received since I did have to sign for it.

The bracelet itself is no dirty wrist grabber. It is old, and it looks to be from the mid-eighteen-hundreds. It is made of tiny rubies surrounded by even tinier clusters of diamonds, and the gold is an ancient, magnificent kind of gold. The bracelet certainly looks its age, which is a marvelous thing in my opinion, as I happen to have a thing for antique jewelry.

The bracelet didn't look very dirty to me when I pulled it out of the purple velvet bag, but then again, people who own antique stuff are often meticulous about it, as they should be. I was instantly dazzled when I saw the bracelet.

I own a jewelry shop right off the French Quarter. I'm far enough away that my little bright blue stucco building costs me far less than it would just a couple of blocks over in any direction, but I'm not so far that both tourists and locals can't find me. I've been doing this for a few years now—okay, I've been fascinated with antique jewelry for my entire life—but I've had the store for three years.

I'm the store's owner and only employee. Unfortunately, it means that when an emergency comes up, or I need a sick day, I have to close. I do have a good online following, though, and a ton of orders for custom-made jewelry come through there—far more than the walk-in traffic I get—so most of the time, it works out okay.

I do close the store on popular auction days and Sundays. I close at six every night, and I don't open until eleven in the morning. I've always had a love for vintage and old things, so the store is full of vintage and antique furniture and artwork. Even the display cabinets are antique. I find most of my jewelry—the antique stuff at any rate—at estate sales, auctions, and online. I don't always get a good deal, but I get what people want. I guess I'm a bit of a middleman in that sense. I don't do that bit for the money, though. I do it because it's a passion, it will always be a passion, and I can't ruin it by calling it work.

The other part of the business is the jewelry I design and make. If you've ever seen the raw kinds of rings, bracelets, necklaces, and earrings on handmade sites or on apps where you can scroll for those kinds of things, that's me. It's what I make. Half the time, the stones look like they've just come out of the earth, though I suppose they've been polished, so maybe not so earthy, but their cut often reminds me of a stone just freshly picked from the dirt, a rare and incredible discovery. Oh, and I also only use ethical stuff. I don't want any bad voodoo in my shop, and I definitely don't want to be putting bad karma into the world. There are enough terrible things going on out there already.

I glance at the pocket watch I always wear around my neck, which I also made. It's a beautiful antique piece from the 1880s. I changed out the chain since it was meant to be fastened to a man's vest or coat, and then I added a few opals set in gold to dangle down beside the watch. I actually designed it to be sold, but once I saw the completed piece, I had to keep it. Opals are my favorite.

The watch is always correct, which is something I love about it. It's ten minutes to noon.

I have to say, the mystery of the dirty wrist grabber—the bracelet—has bothered me all week, and I'm now pretty excited at the prospect of seeing who owns this thing or comes to pick it up who might know the owner. The whole thing even has butterflies exploding in my stomach.

I go to the back to retrieve the bracelet and pull it from the purple velvet bag, where I placed it after it had been cleaned. It's not that I want to touch or ogle it, but well, okay, maybe I do. The thing is worth somewhere between ten and twenty thousand grand—I know because I checked it out after I cleaned it. It's gorgeous, and now that it's all freshly cleaned, it does indeed sparkle in the lights overhead. Any good jewelry store will have good lighting because it makes everything look that much better. It was the one thing I was an absolute stickler about when I bought the tiny building.

A loud thump comes from overhead. I had to do some major soundproofing after I purchased this place because otherwise, the only thing I'd hear all day while I'm trying to work would be the sounds of my four-year-old son being a regular four-year-old. And let me tell you, four-year-old boys can be very, *very* loud.

Milo and his nanny, Charlotte, are upstairs right now. Since it's before noon, they're probably still watching movies or playing with Milo's toys. In the afternoon, Charlotte usually takes him to the park or somewhere fun that isn't indoors, followed by a snack, a nap, then dinner.

The bracelet winks at me as it slithers from the pouch like a white and red snake, curling in the palm of my hand. I stare at it, and suddenly, my mouth goes dry while the overhead lights flicker. I glance up because what the heck is my son doing up there? How can a small child stomp so loudly or jump so fiercely that the lights flicker? Dear lord.

What did the note call this thing? Cursed and dirty. It made me laugh when I read it. Now that it's in the palm of my hand, it feels warm, like it's alive. A shiver crawls up my backbone, which causes goosebumps to pebble my arms and probably my legs too, but those are covered with black leggings, so I can't really tell. I feel cold, though, but the bracelet feels so, so warm in my hand. It feels alive, and it's as if it could go slithering off my palm, onto the floor, and into a vent or something.

But that is a hard no.

Nope. Not having any disasters happen today. No missing bracelets right before the pick-up time because that's not how I roll. I stare down at the bracelet.

"Dirty wrist grabber, or whatever your name is, you behave. You hear me? That's not how I roll here."

Being a bracelet, of course, it has no response.

"You are kind of a pretty thing, though, aren't you?"

I often try on the jewelry sent to me as I have a few good mirrors in the store. But no, I don't do it to be creepy. I do it because I want to make sure I got every spot when I was cleaning. Things can look different when they're worn than they do lying flat on a table or even in my hand.

I know I'm cutting it close, but something tells me I should make sure this thing is immaculate. I pick up the bracelet—yup, it's warm—and place it over my left wrist. I deftly do up the clasp, which isn't easy, but since I've had a lot of practice, I can make quick work of things. Then, I walk over to one of the ornate mirrors I have in my store, where the lighting is best since I specially installed them for my customers to use. Most people probably think the mirror is a cheap replica, but if they look closely, they can tell it's ancient—over two hundred years old. The gold swirl, curlicues, and bent shape of the mirror stare back at me when I lift my wrist.

The lights flicker again.

What in the crazy world? I crank my head up, but there

are no mysterious thumps or bangs that accompany the flicker.

To hell with the weird flickers, I study the bracelet on my wrist from every angle. Now that it's on, it feels lighter than it did in my hand, and it makes me think of things I used to love. Things I haven't let myself think about in a long time—people, or rather, one person in particular. A rugged face, piercing gray eyes, and rich dark hair with red highlights who was quiet, smart, and always worried about someone breaking his heart, so he chose to do the breaking instead.

I shake my head so hard that it nearly rolls right off my shoulders. I have no idea why that face of all faces would come so clearly to me. I mean, I know why, but it's annoying. Normally, I can keep those stuff buried, and actually, I've just reached the point where I don't think about the hurt anymore because I did get something wonderful out of that heartbreak. When I look at Milo, all I see is love even though he has the same dark hair and gray eyes.

Suddenly, the soft tinkle of the bell at the door chimes behind me.

I freeze like I've just been caught licking icing off the edge of a cake in a spot where I think no one would ever see it. *That's something* he *used to do. Holy cakes, he loved cakes. He had an abnormal obsession with cakes.*

That thought tears through my brain with absolutely no subtlety at all while my heart kicks up for no reason. I haven't even turned yet. I should be hustling to the back to get this bracelet off and back in the bag. What if whoever owns it is at the door early?

Fried bananas with whipped cream on pancakes, of course they'd be early. That's just my luck.

"I'll be right with you," I call out as I slowly edge my way along the display counter, closer and closer to the back. I keep myself turned away, just in case.

It's just a few more steps. Just a few. One, two, three, four —just another six or so, and I'll be there. Then I can get the dirty wrist grabber off my wrist and back safely into the purple bag. I imagine myself smiling, thanking whoever is out there for thinking of my store and choosing me, and telling them what an honor it was to handle such a beautiful piece, especially since antique jewelry is one of the great loves of my life. People like it when I say it that way. As though I've had a great many loves.

In reality, I've only ever had one.

Argh! Get out of my head!

How is it possible that I can go for months and months without even thinking about him, but now, my head is all over the place with thoughts I can't control or relegate to the dungeons of my mind? After all, he's nothing more than this abstract idea I usually immediately dismiss because I force it to be that way.

"Take your time. I'm not in a rush."

I freeze, and my heart nearly explodes out of my chest. A volley of goosebumps pricks at my skin while my nipples just about slice through the black lace blouse I'm wearing. I suppose that's what happens when the past hits you all at once. Brick wall, meet my face.

I whirl because it can't be. It. Can't. Be.

But even before I get all the way around, the instant I inhale a steady breath, it's full of cloves and spice, expensive sandalwood, and undertones that smell like a freshly peeled orange.

It can't be, but it is. Once, he was in my heart. This morning, he was in my head. And now, he's here. In my store. Where he absolutely doesn't belong because this is my domain. It's my space, my life, and my work. There isn't any room in it for him. *Anymore*. There isn't any room for him *anymore*.

Those gray eyes—the color of a stormy slate sky right before it opens up and pelts drenching rain down—hit me full force. For a moment, I'm overwhelmed with a sense of loss connected directly to the past. It's like being hit full force with a brick wall again, one that came out of nowhere because I had my head down as I ran straight into the bloody thing. Then, panic. That's what that wall is. I shove it back down, swallowing and breathing hard to regain control of myself. What do people say they do? Find a calm, happy place? I guess I try and do that. I compartmentalize the panic into an imaginary chest and slap a lock on. Those chests are then buried deep inside me. They're rather useful, a great tool to help me sleep at night.

I open my mouth to say his name, but no sound comes out. Those gray orbs sweep to my wrist and widen. His whole face is rugged, like the side of a sexy mountain—the kind of mountain that comes complete with thick forests at the base and is home to mountain goats, bears, and wolves. I used to know every crag, cranny, goat, wolf, and bear that belonged on that mountain—even every tree. Okay, maybe that's taking things too far. The point is, I once had every bit of his face memorized, and it hasn't changed. I watch his lips part. Lips that once had every bit of my body memorized, lips that could subdue me with a single kiss, and lips that created my world and destroyed it, then gave it all back to me again without him even knowing it.

I can't stop myself from staring even though every drop of blood in my entire being surges to my face. Yeah, my face. I'm going with that and ignoring the tingles elsewhere. I'm *not* thinking about how I used to fantasize about this very man when I was with this very man and how he'd work out without a shirt on, and his abs would be all sweaty. The rest of him would be too, but it was his abs, in particular, that would always do me in—his chiseled eight pack covered in droplets of sweat. Okay, whatever. I have weird turn-ons.

I'm also trying very hard not to stare at his body but trying not to stare means staring because he's filling out his dress shirt and slacks in a delicious cupcake sort of way. Not in a soft and squishy way, but just that he's that tasty. I know his pale blue dress shirt is covering muscles—a lot of them. Like bunches, round ones, long ones, and striated, veiny ones.

My eyes lower to his belt against my better judgment, but thank goodness his belt is still above his waistline.

"Why?" he chokes out. I think he means why am I staring, but then he clarifies. "Why are you wearing that?"

"Ahhh!" I squeal as I tug frantically at the bracelet.

My fingers are as useless and stunned as my brain, but thankfully, I have enough practice that habit carries me through. Finally, the clasp gives, so I rush to the back, grab the purple bag, and stuff the bracelet inside. I leave the extra bill for the number of hours I spent cleaning it sitting on the back counter. Then, with a deep breath, I march back out front, drop the bag in the hand of the man who once owned the heart currently beating in my chest like a herd of raging monkeys all vying for a single banana, and clench my teeth together to stop a thousand inappropriate things from springing out.

Or laughter. Because now I can't stop thinking about my heart being the shape of a banana. And monkeys trying to steal it.

"It was sent here for cleaning. I was just making sure I didn't miss anything. Anyway, uh, no charge."

Slate gray eyes narrow at me while heavy, dark brows the same hue as his wild, tousled hair draw together. A single line appears on his broad, strong forehead.

"Um, yeah. It's just...god. I can't believe this belongs to you. I, uh, have another appointment coming right away, though, so if you just want to...yeah. I have to go." I point somewhere behind me. By go, I mean get anywhere but there.

To get away from him, I'd even be willing to go out through the back door of the store right now. I could hide in the bushes back there and watch until he leaves. Then, once he leaves, I'll walk back around the front and lock the door, so I can have a meltdown in private because what the actual fackshit facknuts fackerwacker is happening right now?

I can't help it. I keep staring. Toren has always carried himself with a certain...well...something I don't have. I don't want to say confidence because I might not be made of muscle, have the world's greatest curves, perfect breasts, or a nice round fanny, I might even be a little bit too awkwardly tall for a woman, and if my hair weren't long, it would be stringy and flat because it's so fine, and I don't have chiseled cheekbones or sexy plump lips, but I'm confident enough. My hair is jet black, which is all-natural, and my skin is kind of on the pale side, giving me an authentic unnatural look that some people would no doubt term as gothic if I helped it along with makeup, but that's okay with me.

Holy gravy with a side of biscuits, I'm rambling—thought rambling.

We're both standing there stunned when the lights flicker again. I grind my teeth and stare upward like the ceiling is going to cave in. There's a great bang upstairs, then a thump, thump, thump, which is dull and barely discernable, but I know what it is. I need to get to the back stairs, to the door I don't keep locked since it goes up to my apartment.

Suddenly, there's a clomp, clomp, clomp.

Oh goodness, for the love of monkeys and banana hearts, please, just no.

But there they are. While I'm frozen to the floor like an ice statue, Milo and Charlotte walk down.

"Sorry," Charlotte says as soon as she sees me. She must not realize my face is contorted into a million signals of "*please take Milo back upstairs right freaking now!!!*" because she continues to tell me how they were playing a game of don't touch the floor. She explains how there were a few instances when they fell, which caused the bangs, then she apologizes for the disruption and adds that they might have smashed the coffee table and put a hole through the flat-screen TV all in one shot.

My mouth drops.

And the mouth that belongs to the man who broke my heart also drops.

Because he's basically staring at a mini-me. His mini-me.

Milo's mouth drops open too, and he freezes. He was sheepish and guilty and worried about the TV, which is seriously the tenth one he's managed to break in the past three years—how is that even possible?—but now he's looking at a bigger version of himself. One with gray eyes and dark sandy hair.

Both sets of steel-gray eyes dart to my face, and also one set of warm brown ones since Charlotte is noticing the same thing as them.

"Lu?" He breaks my name down like he has a right to it, but it's no endearment. It's a question.

Okay, so I never told Toren Cromwell, the ex-love of my

life and the eighth wonder of the world with chiseled six-pack sweaty abs worth fantasizing over, that he's a dad.

Shit, shit, shit, biscuits with a side of shit biscuits, I have a feeling my banana heart is about to get peeled wide open.

Ex for You
Available on Amazon

ABOUT THE AUTHOR

Lindsey Hart specializes in sweet to extra hot and dirty romances and strongly believes in happily ever after. If you are looking for a page turner, then you are in for a wild and naughty ride with feisty heroines and alpha male heroes. Full list of her books is available on Amazon.

Printed in Great Britain
by Amazon

64645390R00122